The Book of Everything

The Book of

Everything

a *novel by* **Guus Kuijer**

Translated by John Nieuwenhuizen

ARTHUR A. LEVINE BOOKS

An Imprint of Scholastic Inc.

Text copyright © 2004 by Guus Kuijer
Translation copyright © 2006 by John Nieuwenhuizen
All rights reserved. Published by Arthur A. Levine Books,
an imprint of Scholastic Inc., *Publishers since 1920*,
by arrangement with Em. Querido's Uitgeverij B.V.,
Amsterdam, the Netherlands.

SCHOLASTIC and the LANTERN LOGO are
trademarks and/or registered trademarks of Scholastic Inc.

For information regarding permission, write to Scholastic Inc.,
Attention: Permissions Department,
557 Broadway, New York, NY 10012.

Library of Congress Cataloging-in-Publication Data
Kuijer, Guus, 1942-
[Boek van alle dingen. English]
The book of everything / by Guus Kuijer ; translated by John Nieuwenhuizen.—1st ed.
p. cm.
Summary: Nine-year-old Thomas receives encouragement from many sources, including candid
talks with Jesus, to help him tolerate the strict family life dictated by his deeply religious father.
ISBN 0-439-74918-2
[1. Family problems—Fiction 2. Christian life—Fiction. 3. Amsterdam (Netherlands)—
Fiction.] I. Nieuwenhuizen, John. II. Title.
PZ7.K9490143Boo 2006
[Fic]—dc22 2005018717

10 9 8 7 6 5 4 3 2 1   06 07 08 09 10

Printed in the United States of America   37
First American edition, April 2006

Historical Note

In 1951, when this book begins, the Netherlands was still struggling with the consequences of its occupation by Germany during World War II. Germany invaded the Netherlands on May 10, 1940, and dominated the country for almost exactly five years, surrendering on May 6, 1945. In that time, some Dutch people collaborated with the Nazis and assisted in their operations; many others fought bravely in the Resistance to shelter Jews and thwart the Nazi regime.

Before the Story Begins...

I think it's okay to tell you: This business with Thomas was quite unexpected for me too. I had really wanted to write quite a different book. A book that was moving, but also made you laugh. It was going to be about my happy childhood. About my father, who played his violin for me so beautifully before I went to bed. About my mother, who sang so sweetly. So movingly! About my brothers and sisters, who worshipped me. About my friends, who came to share the cake on my birthday. It was going to be called *The Adventures of a Happy Child*. I imagined how it would be a favorite Christmas gift. Not just children, but fathers and mothers, grandparents, and even the prime minister would read it in a single sitting. Preferably by candlelight, in front of a crackling wood fire and accompanied by a mug of hot chocolate.

But then I received a visit from Mr. Klopper. I didn't know him. He didn't know me either, but he knew who I was because I am a world-famous writer of children's books. I say this in all humility.

Mr. Klopper was exactly the same age as me. His hair was

white and the top of his head nearly bald. But Mr. Klopper, too, had once been a child.

When we were sitting together in front of my crackling wood fire, Mr. Klopper produced a thick exercise book from his bag. "I know you as a writer with a great feeling for your fellow human beings," he said.

I nodded, because that was true. I have enormous feeling for my fellow human beings. I could do with a bit less, actually.

"That is why I wanted you to read this." He handed me the exercise book. "I wrote this when I was nine," he told me. "I reread it lately. I think it is worthwhile. But I think you should read it first, because it may be too disrespectful."

This shocked me. "Disrespectful?" I said.

"Yes," said Mr. Klopper. "I had an unhappy childhood, and that makes you disrespectful."

I stared into the crackling wood fire. Disrespectfulness is a problem, especially in children's books. "I'll have a look at it," I said. "I'll let you know."

I saw Mr. Klopper out. "Are you still disrespectful these days?" I asked him in the doorway.

Mr. Klopper nodded.

"At your age?"

"That's how it is," he said, and disappeared into the thickly falling snow.

That same day, I read *The Book of Everything* in one sitting. It was indeed disrespectful. I myself am a very respectful person, but it is easy for me to talk. I had a happy childhood. That wonderful school, every day of the week. My teachers: Mr. Sawtooth! Miss Knitpin! Every evening, my father's dulcet violin and my mother's sweet soprano! I don't have a single reason to be disrespectful, but unhappy children have their rights too, I think.

I called Mr. Klopper, and we arranged a meeting. Together, we spent many an evening in front of my crackling wood fire, and that is how this book came to be.

"Well, Thomas?" I asked the final evening. "Did you manage to do it?" For by this time we were on first-name terms.

"What, Guus?"

"Did you become happy?"

"Yes," he said.

And we drank a mug of hot chocolate.

Thomas saw things no one else could see. He didn't know why, but it had always been like that. He could remember a violent hailstorm one day. Thomas leapt into a doorway and watched the leaves being ripped from the trees. He ran home.

"It's autumn all of a sudden," he shouted. "All the leaves have gone from the trees."

His mother looked out of the window. "Of course they haven't. What on earth makes you think that?"

Thomas could see she was right. The trees were still covered in leaves. "Not here," he said. "But in Jan van Eyck Street all the leaves are on the ground."

"Oh, I see," said his mother. He could tell from her face that she didn't believe him.

Thomas went up to his room and took out the book he was writing. *The Book of Everything*, it was called. He picked up his pen and wrote. "It was hailing so hard that the leaves were ripped from the trees. This really happened, in Jan van Eyck Street in Amsterdam, when I was nine, in the summer of 1951."

He looked out of the window to think, because without a window he couldn't think. Or maybe it was the other way around: When there was a window, he automatically started to think. Then he wrote, "When I grow up, I am going to be happy."

He heard his father coming home and thought, "It is half past five and I still don't know what my book is about. What are books about, anyway?"

He asked this question during dinner.

"About love and things," giggled his sister, Margot, who went to high school and was dumb as an ox.

But Father said, "All important books are about God."

"They are about God as well as about love," said Mother, but Father glared at her so sternly it made her flush.

"Who reads books in this family?" he asked.

"You do," she said.

"So who should know what books are about, you or I?"

"You," said Mother.

"When I grow up, I'm going to be happy," Thomas thought, but he didn't say it out loud. He looked at his mother and could see that she was sad. He wanted to get up and throw his arms around her, but he couldn't do that. He didn't know why, but it was simply not possible. He stayed where he was, in his chair.

Margot giggled again. That was because she was so dumb.

"It was hailing so hard in Jan van Eyck Street that the leaves were ripped from the trees," he said aloud.

Mother looked at him and smiled. It was as if he had thrown his arms around her after all, she looked so happy.

"This is a secret message only Mama understands," he thought. That must be true, because Father and Margot didn't look up from their plates.

When Mother was tucking him in, she asked, "Are you going to have wonderful dreams, my little dreamer?"

Thomas nodded. "Do you think I'm a bit nice?" he asked.

"You're the nicest boy in the whole world," she said. She wrapped her arms around him and hugged him. Thomas could feel she was crying a little. He went ice-cold inside and thought, "God will punish Father terribly, with bubonic plague or something."

But later, when he lay staring into the dark all alone, he grew afraid that God might be angry with him. He said, "I can't help it if I think things. And I don't mean it, so it's not really bad. I don't even know what bubonic plague is."

Then he fell asleep.

It had been so boiling hot for a week that there were tropical fish swimming in the canals. Thomas had seen them with his own eyes. They were swordtails. He knew that for sure because he had swordtails in his aquarium. They're cute little fish that do a funny dance in the water when they're in love.

It was not far from the girls' high school where Margot went. He was lying flat on his stomach in the grass at the water's edge on Reijnier Vinkeles Quay and saw them swimming past. Dozens at a time. As he was walking home, he wondered if anyone was going to believe him. Then he met Eliza, who was sixteen. She was in the same class as Margot and lived around the corner. She had an artificial leg made of leather, which creaked like a new pair of shoes.

"There are tropical fish swimming in the canal," he said.

Eliza stopped, so her leg stopped creaking.

Thomas felt a kind of electric shock, because he suddenly realized how lovely she was.

"That's because people flush them down the toilet when they go on vacation," she said.

For a moment, Thomas could not think, because Eliza kept looking at him with her dark blue eyes. "And because of the heat," he stuttered.

"Actually, there are crocodiles living in the sewer too," said Eliza. She walked on, so her leg started creaking again.

Thomas followed her. "Really?" he asked. "Have you seen them yourself?"

"One of them," said Eliza. "The size of my little finger. In the toilet." She held up her hand.

Thomas was shocked, because the hand only had its fourth finger. The rest of the fingers weren't there.

"Oh," he said. He waited till Eliza had turned the corner. He felt the shock deep in his stomach. But in his head merry bells were ringing. "She is lovely," he thought. "And she understands what I see. She understands that what I see is really there. So Eliza knows it too."

He walked home, wondering, "What does Eliza know?" It was hard trying to think without a window to look through. "I can't explain what Eliza knows, but I know it too: that there is something strange about me." And when he was home, sitting in front of his window, he thought, "Where could her other fingers have gone?"

"Sunday is the only day you have to push like a handcart," Thomas wrote in *The Book of Everything*. "The other days roll down the bridge by themselves."

On Sundays, they went to church. Not to an ordinary church in the neighborhood, but to a special church a long way from home. It was a church in an ordinary house, without a steeple. During the service, you could hear the people upstairs doing the vacuum cleaning. Hardly anybody went to that church, but his family all did: Father, Mother, Margot, and Thomas. Mother wore a hat and Margot a scarf over her hair, because they had to in church. You weren't allowed to see the women's hairdos. For men it didn't matter, because they didn't have hairdos.

They walked, because God did not want trams to run on Sundays. The trams ran anyway, and that was not very nice for God to have to put up with.

There were two most shameful things. One was having been on the wrong side in the War. The other: riding in a tram on a Sunday.

Thomas simply thought the trams away. He thought away everything that was forbidden: the trams, the cars, the bicycles, and the boys playing soccer in the street. The birds could stay, for they didn't know it was Sunday. Because they had no soul.

The church service was attended by about twenty ancient people who were deaf or blind or lame. And if there was nothing else wrong with them, they had at least two warts growing on their chins. Apart from Thomas and Margot, there were two other children. Two sisters. They were so pale under their headscarves they would obviously die soon. "I give them till 1955," Thomas wrote in *The Book of Everything*. "By then they will be dead and buried. May they rest in peace for all eternity." He wrote these words with a lump in his throat because it was so sad for those children. But unfortunately there was nothing to be done about it.

The service took a long time. The children of Israel

dragged themselves murmuring through the wilderness and the pews were hard.

The good bit was the singing back and forth. That went like this:

A bald gentleman in a long black dress with lots of small buttons sang a line by himself. Then the people had to sing a line back all together. Again and again. Turn and turn about. The black dress sang something different every time, but the people always responded with the same line.

"Musical Lord, forgive our miserable singing."

Thomas joined in at the top of his voice. He tried to count the buttons on the black dress at the same time, but he kept losing count.

On the way home, Thomas noticed that Father was cross about something. Father said nothing and looked straight ahead. At the table, after the prayer, he said, "Thomas, stand up."

Thomas was just about to put a forkful of potato and peas into his mouth. His fork stayed halfway up.

"Stand up?" he said.

"Stand up," said Father.

"Why?" Mother asked, worried.

"Because I say so," replied Father.

"Oh, that is why," said Margot.

Thomas put his fork down on his plate and stood up.

"Hee hee hee," Margot giggled, because she was as dumb as an onion. You couldn't understand how she kept getting eighties and nineties in all her classes.

"Let us hear what you were singing during the litany," said Father with a stern look on his face. The litany was the singing back and forth in church.

Thomas looked at his mother.

"Look at me and sing," said Father.

Thomas took a deep breath and sang: "Musical Lord, forgive our miserable singing."

Then it became terribly quiet. Before his eyes, Thomas saw a black dress with more than a thousand little buttons. Two sparrows on the windowsill were playing bright trumpets, because they didn't know it was Sunday.

Mother said, "He is only nine. He doesn't do it deliberately."

Father was silent. Solemnly, he put his fork and knife down on his plate and stood up. He grew taller and taller until his head was higher than the lamp over the table.

Every living thing on earth held its breath. The sparrows on the windowsill choked on their trumpets. The sun went dark and the sky shrank.

"What are you doing?" Mother cried. She jumped up and pulled Thomas back.

"Go away, woman," Father roared. "I am speaking to your son."

But Mother pulled Thomas farther away from the table and put her arms around his shoulders.

Then Father's hand flashed out suddenly and slapped her on the cheek. She staggered back and let go of Thomas.

The angels in heaven covered their eyes with their hands and sobbed loudly, because that is what they always do when a man hits his wife. A profound sadness settled over the earth.

"Papa," whispered Margot.

"Silence!" Father thundered. "Thomas, upstairs. And don't forget the spoon."

Thomas turned, went to the kitchen, and pulled the wooden spoon from the spoon rack. Then he ran upstairs to his room. He sat down by the window and stared out, but he couldn't manage to think. The world was empty. Everything there had ever been had been thought away by someone. There was only sound. He heard the slap smack into his mother's soft cheek. He heard all the slaps Mother had ever suffered, a rain of slaps, as if it was hailing in Jan van Eyck Street and the leaves were being ripped off the trees. He pressed his hands over his ears.

When Thomas had been looking at nothing for an eternity, he heard, right through his hands, his father walking heavily up the stairs. *Thump, thump. Thump, thump.*

"Everything is gone," he thought. "Nothing exists any longer. I don't either."

Thump, thump. Thump, thump.

There he was. The man appeared like a tree in the doorway. He came up to Thomas and held out his hand. Thomas gave him the wooden spoon. Then the man sat down on the stool next to Thomas's bed. He did not say anything. There was no need, for Thomas knew exactly what he had to do. He took off his trousers. Then his underpants. He lay facedown across his father's knees, his bare bottom up.

The hitting began. The wooden spoon swished through the air.

Thwack!

The pain cut through his skin like a knife.

Thwack!

At first, Thomas thought of nothing, but, after the third hit, words came into his head.

Thwack! God . . .

Thwack! will . . .

Thwack! punish . . .

Thwack! him . . .

Thwack! terribly . . .

Thwack! with . . .

Thwack! all . . .

Thwack! the . . .

Thwack! plagues . . .

Thwack! of . . .

Thwack! Egypt . . .

Thwack! because . . .

Thwack! he . . .

Thwack! hit . . .

Thwack! Mama. . . .

The sentence was finished, but the hitting went on. For a moment, his head was empty. But then they came again: terrible words, words he had never thought before:

Thwack! God . . .

Thwack! does . . .

Thwack! not . . .

Thwack! exist. . . .

Thwack! God . . .

Thwack! does . . .

Thwack! not . . .

Thwack! exist. . . .

When at last the hitting stopped and he pulled his underpants and trousers up over his fiery bottom, he knew that the Heavenly Father had been beaten out of him forever.

"Merciful Lord," said Father. "Repeat after me."

"Merciful Lord," said Thomas.

"Forgive us miserable sinners," said Father.

"Forgive us miserable sinners," said Thomas.

"You stay up here," said Father. "You'll repeat this sentence properly one hundred times and then you will come down." He stumbled down the stairs. *Thump, thump. Thump, thump.*

Thomas stayed standing up because his bottom felt like a pincushion. He stared out of the window and whispered, "Please, God, will you please exist. All the plagues of Egypt, please. He has hit Mama and it wasn't the first time!"

God was silent in every language. The angels tried to dry their tears, but their handkerchiefs were so soaked through that it started raining even in the deserts.

2

Next door to Thomas lived an old lady. All the children in the neighborhood knew she was a witch. She lived by herself, and all her dresses were black. She wore her hair done up in a gray bun and she had two black cats. Once a week she went out to do her shopping, but all the other days she stayed at home to brew her magic potions.

Because she was a witch, children pestered her. They banged on her windows or pushed filthy stuff through her letterbox. But when Eliza-with-the-leather-leg saw this, she became angry and ran creaking after the children. "Leave her in peace," she shouted. "You ought to know better."

Thomas left her in peace. He knew better. In *The Book of Everything* he wrote:

"On Wednesday the fifth of September 1951, Mrs. van Amersfoort put a spell on the Bottombiter."

This is what happened:

Every so often, a large black dog stormed into the street. No one knew where he came from or where he lived. He just appeared, big, mean, and savage. All the children ran home screaming, but the Bottombiter always managed to get one or two of them. With his huge, growling teeth, he would bite their bottoms. And then he was gone. Where? Nowhere. He was just gone, until, a few weeks later, he appeared again.

On the fifth of September, old Mrs. van Amersfoort, who, as everyone knew, was a witch, was lugging her heavy shopping bag home. It was a fine day. Lots of children were playing in the street. Suddenly, they started screaming, because the Bottombiter was bounding up the street, all his teeth bared.

Thomas tried to run home, but Mrs. van Amersfoort got in the way. So he stopped right behind her and stood very still. The Bottombiter came straight at her. Thomas pressed his hands protectively against his bottom.

"Stop!" Mrs. van Amersfoort shouted sternly.

She dropped her shopping bag on the sidewalk with a thud and raised her hands, making her look much taller than she really was.

"Stop!" she repeated.

The Bottombiter stopped in surprise and looked up at her hands.

Then Mrs. van Amersfoort started whispering things. They were obviously magic spells, but Thomas couldn't understand them.

The Bottombiter whined softly and wagged his tail timidly.

Mrs. van Amersfoort lowered her hands, but her mouth muttered on.

First, the Bottombiter sat, then he lay down, and finally rolled over onto his back with his four big paws up in the air.

Mrs. van Amersfoort left him like that for a while, looking down on him silently.

Thomas was the only one to see it, because the other children had all run inside.

"Good dog," said Mrs. van Amersfoort. "Off home now."

The Bottombiter rose and crept down the street, his tail between his legs.

Mrs. van Amersfoort reached for her bag, but it was so heavy she could hardly get it off the ground.

Then Thomas heard a ringing in his ears and asked, "Would you like me to carry your bag inside?" He'd said it without even thinking, shocking himself.

Mrs. van Amersfoort, who really was a witch, looked at him seriously.

The ringing changed into music of a kind Thomas had never heard before, with lots of violins. His heart was thumping anxiously and he hoped desperately that Mrs. van Amersfoort would say no.

"Yes, please," she said. "That's very kind of you." She unlocked the front door.

The music had stopped and Thomas started tugging at the bag, but he couldn't lift it even a centimeter off the ground. It felt as if it were chock-full of rocks.

Mrs. van Amersfoort didn't notice. "It won't be heavy for you," she called as she walked into the house. "You're such a big boy already."

She had barely finished speaking when his ears started ringing again and the bag rose slowly off the sidewalk. It was still heavy, but a lot less so than it had been at first.

Mrs. van Amersfoort had disappeared into the darkness of the hallway. In the distance, a light flicked on. "Just put it down here," she called. Thomas saw her standing by the sink in the kitchen. "Would you like a glass of cordial?"

"Yes, please," said Thomas. His heart was thumping because Mrs. van Amersfoort was a witch, and so her kitchen must be a witch's kitchen.

The cordial was as red as blood.

"Sit down in the living room," said Mrs. van Amersfoort. "I'll be right there."

Thomas stepped into the room and took a look around. The glass with bloodred cordial shook in his hand. He thought, "Don't mind the mess," because that was what Mother always said when there was a visitor. At home, there never was a mess, but here there was. The chairs, the tables, and the floor were covered in stacks of newspapers, magazines, and books. Along the walls stood bookshelves full of books stacked higgledy-piggledy. In one corner stood a huge globe with a black cat lying fast asleep on top. Pinned to one of the shelves was a map on which someone had roughly drawn some arrows. A large bird with spread wings was suspended from the ceiling.

Now Thomas knew for sure that it was true. This was the house of a witch. But he was not sure if it was the sinister house of a sinister witch. That remained to be seen.

"I'll be right there," Mrs. van Amersfoort called from the kitchen. "Clear yourself a chair."

Carefully, Thomas put his glass on a low table between a photo album and a pile of books. He lifted a stack of papers from a chair with carved legs and sat down. A black cat appeared from under a cupboard. It meowed as it approached Thomas, its tail standing straight up, and rubbed against Thomas's legs. The cat on top of the globe woke up and gave him a drowsy look.

Then Mrs. van Amersfoort came in. "There we are, a cup of coffee for me," she said, clearing a chair and sitting down. She regarded Thomas contentedly. "I think it's damned nice that you're here," she said.

Thomas was shocked by the word "damned." With his friends he swore all the time, because he went to the Biblical Christian School, but this was the first time he'd heard an adult swear.

"My children all left home long ago, and my husband . . ."

Mrs. van Amersfoort sipped her coffee and looked Thomas in the eyes.

"Of course, you wouldn't know," she said. "You were too young at the time. They executed my husband."

Thomas said, "Oh," because he didn't understand what she meant.

"'Executed' means they shot him dead with guns," said Mrs. van Amersfoort. "The Nazis did. He was in the Resistance during the war, you know."

Thomas nodded. "Oh, I see," he said.

He felt a great sadness in his throat and in his stomach. The same kind of sadness as when, again and again, year after year, they nailed Jesus to the Cross. He was always glad when it was over again and the Lord had risen, safe and sound, from His grave.

"Don't be sad," said Mrs. van Amersfoort. She got up and pointed at a small blue case. "Here, have you seen one of those before?" She folded back the lid of the case.

Thomas nodded. It was a portable gramophone.

"I'll let you listen to something," she said. She vigorously turned a handle and then put on a record.

Music drifted into the room from far, far away. It was music Thomas had never heard before, with lots of violins. The sadness melted away from his throat and from his stomach. Thomas closed his eyes and there, in the dark behind his eyelids, suddenly appeared the Lord Jesus. Thomas was scared out of his wits, but he kept his eyes closed, because he was curious to know what the Lord would have to say.

Jesus smiled and said, "I'll never let myself be nailed to the Cross again, I just won't. I've had enough of it."

Then He disappeared, as quickly as He had come.

That was good news, particularly for Mr. Onstein at school. He would never have to tell that terrible story again. Thomas felt intensely happy.

"Beautiful, isn't it?" Mrs. van Amersfoort whispered.

"Yes," said Thomas. His ears started ringing again. The globe started spinning, cat and all. When he was about to draw Mrs. van Amersfoort's attention to this, he saw that her heavy chair was floating above the floor like a low cloud. He barely had time to take this in when he felt the chair with the carved legs he was sitting in rising slowly, as if strong hands were lifting it. He wanted to shout with joy, but when he saw Mrs. van Amersfoort's intent face, he realized that, with this music, it was normal for chairs to float.

"Beethoven," Mrs. van Amersfoort whispered. "When I listen to this . . ." She didn't finish her sentence. There was no need, for Thomas knew exactly what she wanted to say, even though he could not find words for it. His mind wandered off and he could see himself floating above green meadows and a castle with a Rolls-Royce parked in front. A wondrously beautiful princess waved to him with a white hand-kerchief. She had a leather leg that creaked when she walked, and she wore a sky-blue dress with a white collar. Her father stood on the terrace playing the violin while her mother sang sweetly.

The record came to an end and started making a scratching noise. Thomas was startled. *Bump!* The chairs landed gently on the carpet. "Did Mrs. van Amersfoort notice we were floating?" he wondered. He didn't know and waited to see if she would say something, but she didn't. She was staring into the distance. Perhaps she was thinking of her husband who had been shot dead with guns.

Thomas took a sip of cordial and said, "You have such a lot of books. What are they all about?"

"Heavens," Mrs. van Amersfoort exclaimed. "What are books about? They are about everything that exists. Do you like reading?"

Thomas nodded.

"Hold on," said Mrs. van Amersfoort. "I may have something for you." She turned to one of the bookshelves. "What do you want to be when you grow up?"

"Happy," said Thomas. "When I grow up, I am going to be happy."

Mrs. van Amersfoort was about to pull a book from the shelf, but turned in surprise. She looked at Thomas with a smile and said, "That is a damn good idea. And do you know how happiness begins? It begins with no longer being afraid."

She pulled the book from the shelf. "Here you are," she said.

Thomas felt himself flush. He stared at the book on his lap. *Emil and the Detectives,* it was called.

"Thank you very much," he stammered.

"It's about a boy who does not want to be afraid, and who fights the injustice in the world," Mrs. van Amersfoort explained. "You can keep it."

She finished her coffee and Thomas his cordial.

"You've been very brave today," she said. "You've come in even though all the children say I am a witch."

Thomas didn't dare look at her. She knew! She said it just like that, straight to his face.

"They're right, of course," she said. "I am a witch."

It became dead quiet. So quiet Thomas could hear Father shouting and Mother wailing, clean through the wall. "Goodness," he said. "It's after half past five. I have to get home." He jumped up with his book in his hand. "Good-bye. And thank you."

He walked out of the room, but stopped at the front door. Had he thanked Mrs. van Amersfoort sufficiently? No. He returned to the room. "For everything," he said.

"That's all right, my boy," said Mrs. van Amersfoort. "You won't be afraid anymore, will you?"

"No," said Thomas. "Not of witches, anyway."

3

When he walked into the living room, clutching his book, Father and Mother were sitting at the table in silence. Mother's housekeeping book lay open in front of them. That was where she wrote down all the things she bought and how much everything had cost.

"I really must get dinner going now," she said.

"No," said Father. "First we have to finish this."

He checked the housekeeping book, one purchase after the other. He had a red pencil in his hand.

"Hello, Thomas," said Mother.

She turned her cheek toward him, but Thomas said, "The other cheek, Mama."

"Why?" she asked.

"Because," said Thomas.

He saw her flush. Then she turned her right cheek toward him. He kissed it. It was the cheek that had been hit.

"Where did you get that book?" asked Father. He wrote figures on a sheet of paper, one underneath the other.

"From Mrs. van Amersfoort."

Father looked up. He took off his glasses and looked at

Thomas absently. "So you met Mrs. van Amersfoort and she said, 'Here you are, have this book'?"

"No, that's not how it went," said Thomas.

"So how did it go?"

"I carried her shopping bag in for her."

"That was nice of you!" Mother exclaimed. "That poor woman is so alone. . . ."

Father put his glasses back on and continued his figuring. "I would rather you did not go there," he said

There was a silence. The clock on the mantelpiece struck six. Thomas looked at the copper geckoes that climbed up the chimney-piece toward the ceiling.

"But why not?" Mother asked softly.

"That woman is a Communist, you know that perfectly well," said Father. "When the Russians come, she'll be out on the sidewalk cheering. And all of us Christians will become slaves."

There was another silence. The veranda doors stood open and you could hear the neighbors talking and laughing in their gardens. A wave of music floated into the room.

"Isn't that lovely," Mother whispered. "Beethoven . . . *All men will be brothers . . .*"

"Let me have a look at that book," said Father.

Thomas put it down on the table.

"*Emil and the Detectives,*" Father read out. "By Erich Kaestner. He is a Communist too, I think."

"It's only a children's book," said Mother. "What harm could it do?"

Father pushed the book across the table at Thomas. "Take it back as soon as possible," he said. "And don't ever go in there again."

"Can I go and start dinner now?" asked Mother.

"But how do you think you will get to the end of this month?" Father asked.

"I'll make it up out of my clothes allowance," said Mother.

"No, no, that's going a bit far," he said. Sighing, he pulled his wallet from his back pocket and took out a twenty-five-guilder note. "Here, take this," he said. "But do try to manage on the housekeeping money."

Thomas crept out of the room with his book. Mother went into the kitchen, the twenty-five-guilder note in her hand.

"Dear Eliza," Thomas wrote in *The Book of Everything*. "Maybe you think you are not beautiful because you have a leather leg that creaks when you walk. Or because one of your hands has only a little finger and nothing else. But that is not true. You are the most beautiful girl in the world. I think that later you are going to live in a castle with a Rolls-Royce in the driveway. I do not write this because I want to go out with you, for you are already sixteen and I am only nine (nearly ten), so that is not possible. I write it because it is true."

He stared out of the window and thought, "What a pity I don't dare write this to Eliza."

Pity, pity, pity, for it was a lovely letter, particularly that bit about the castle and the Rolls-Royce. "I won't dare, never in my life, no way."

"Do you know how happiness begins?" Mrs. van Amersfoort said in his head. "It begins with no longer being afraid."

That was easy for her to say, because she was a witch. But wait a minute. Perhaps she had become a witch *because* she was no longer afraid.

Thomas found a sheet of paper and wrote: "Dear Eliza, I actually don't have the courage to write this, but I'm doing it all the same. . . ." Then he copied his letter, castle, Rolls-Royce, and all. He folded the paper twice and slid it into an envelope. "For Eliza," he wrote on it in beautiful script with lots of flourishes. He put the envelope into his trouser pocket. Maybe, just maybe, he would one day give it to Eliza. You never knew.

"Thomas, Margot, dinner is ready," Mother called from downstairs.

He met Margot in the hall. "What was it like in there?" she asked.

"Where?" asked Thomas.

"At the witch's place."

Thomas suddenly thought that the word "witch" sounded

nasty. He had to swallow before he could say, "How should I know?"

They went down the stairs. "I know perfectly well that you've been there," Margot hissed. Before they reached the living room door, she grabbed him by the scruff of the neck. "Come on, tell me. What was it like in there?"

He looked her in the face. How could he explain to an onion what it was like at Mrs. van Amersfoort's? "It was . . . ah . . . different," he said.

Margot shook him. "Different from what?"

"Different from our place," Thomas said.

She let go of him. "I'll talk to you later," she said.

They went into the room. Father and Mother were already at the table. The pots stood steaming under the light. Thomas could smell it right away: potatoes, cauliflower, and meat. He didn't like cauliflower.

They sat down.

"Let us pray," said Father.

They folded their hands and closed their eyes.

"O Lord our God," Father began.

"Hey there, Thomas," Thomas heard in his head. In the dark behind his eyelids he saw Jesus in a long white dress that flapped in the breeze. "How's it going, my boy?" Jesus asked.

"Good," said Thomas.

"Just good or Beethoven good?"

"Just good," said Thomas. "But . . ." He didn't dare go on.

"No need to be afraid, lad," said Jesus. "You can tell me. I won't tell anyone. Word of honor." The Lord Jesus spat in His right hand and raised two fingers.

"He must not hit Mama," said Thomas. He felt his eyes fill with tears, but he didn't want to cry.

"Who must not hit Mama?" Jesus asked.

"You know perfectly well," Thomas said angrily.

"Blank's my name," said Jesus.

"How odd," thought Thomas. "Granddad always says, 'Blank's my name,' and no one else does."

"I mean," said Jesus, "that I know nothing about it."

"Papa, of course," Thomas cried.

Jesus said nothing, but you could see in His face how shocked He was. And sad and angry too. "Well, I'll be. . . ." He said then. "Has he gone completely off his head?!"

That last expression was one of Aunt Pie's!

But then Thomas heard his father say, "In the name of our Lord Jesus Christ, amen."

Thomas opened his eyes, and Jesus was gone.

"Enjoy the meal," said Mother.

Father cut the meat. The knife slid through the meat as if it were foam. But it wasn't, because you could see blood oozing from it.

"Isn't that knife razor-sharp, Papa!" said Margot.

"Yes," said Father proudly, "I sharpen it every week."

"It cuts clean through everything, no matter how tough!" said Margot.

"That's right," said Father. "You could butcher an old cow with it."

"Rip, rip, right through it," said Margot, her eyes glistening.

Father shared out the meat, giving himself the largest piece, because he had to work so hard in the office. "I dislike blunt knives," he said.

That evening, when Mother was putting Thomas to bed, she whispered, "Mrs. van Amersfoort's husband gave his life for our freedom. She saved people herself, too, during the war. I'll always let you visit her, but just make sure Papa doesn't notice."

"Okay, Mama. Mama?"

"Yes?"

"Are you happy?"

"Yes, my own boy, because you make me happy." She kissed him, switched off the light, and went downstairs.

Thomas thought about what Mother had said. That he didn't have to obey Father, as long as he did it secretly. And that she was happy. He had the feeling that something was not right, but he couldn't quite work out what.

4

Thomas was worried, because he had taken the plunge. He had put his letter into Eliza's letterbox. What was he going to do if he met her? Which way would he look? The best thing would be to hide himself and never reappear. That was why he was at home, reading *Emil and the Detectives*. It was a wonderful book about a German boy in Berlin. It was not about God. It seemed Emil never had to go to church, which was odd.

When he had read for half an hour, he put the book down with a sigh. Perhaps it would be okay to go outside for a bit, if he was really careful. If he saw Eliza, he could for instance quickly jump into a doorway, or hide behind a fat lady, just like Emil in Berlin. As he was going down the stairs to the front door, he saw a white envelope lying on the doormat at the bottom of the stairs. His mouth became dry from nervousness, for that letter was from Eliza, he was convinced of it. If it was an angry letter, he did not want to go on living. He would go and drown himself in the Reijnier Vinkeles Canal, among the swordtails.

With thudding heart he went down one tread at a time and picked up the envelope from the mat. "To Mr. A. Klopper," read the address. That was Father, for Thomas's name was T. Klopper. And on the back: "Mrs. van Amersfoort-Raaphorst."

It wasn't a letter from Eliza at all! It was a letter from Mrs. van Amersfoort to his father! That was even worse! That was a national disaster! Quickly he stuffed the envelope under his shirt. He looked up into the dark stairwell. No one had seen him. Carefully he opened and closed the door. He ran down the street, turned the corner, and kept running until he reached somewhere where no one knew him. Then he stopped, gasping for breath.

He examined the letter in his hand. Why would Mrs. van Amersfoort write a letter to his father? This could only lead to trouble. Father must never get that letter. He must tear it up and bury it, for Mrs. van Amersfoort was a commernist or something, and a witch on top of that. And who would get the blame if his father received a letter from that woman? He! Thomas! And nobody else. He clasped the letter in his hands and was about to start tearing it up when he thought, "I wonder what's in it?" He could read the letter first and then tear it up, couldn't he? Then he would at least know what it was about!

He looked around to make sure no one was watching him. Carefully, he undid the envelope. Why were his fingers trembling so? Why did his stomach feel as if he had swallowed a rhinoceros? Because he was doing something that was totally forbidden. "But," he thought, "it has to be done, because if I don't, much worse things are likely to happen." What sort of things? "For instance somebody could get a terrible belting and that person could for instance be me."

He pulled the letter from the envelope and unfolded it. There was only a single sentence. Thomas read it aloud to himself: "*A man who hits his wife dishonors himself.*"

"A man who hits his wife . . ." Thomas muttered uneasily. So she knew! He flushed with shame. She had discovered the great secret. There were secrets you could safely pass on. But this was a secret that nobody must know, because it was awful. Mrs. van Amersfoort knew it. How could that be? Had someone told her or did she just know, automatically, because she was a witch?

". . . dishonors himself," he mumbled. What did "dishonors" mean? He had no idea.

"Papa must not ever read this," he whispered. "For I will be blamed for it, and probably Mama too."

He walked over to the Van Heutz monument. In front of the monument was a pond with a fountain where children sailed small boats. Behind it grew shrubs. He slipped in among the shrubs, squatted, and started digging a hole in the ground with his hands. He stuffed the envelope into the hole, but when he was about to put the letter in too, he hesitated. Once more, he reread the sentence Mrs. van Amersfoort had written. *A man who hits his wife dishonors himself.* He thought. Perhaps it was a magic spell. A spell that could change people into ... eh ... something. That was quite possible. He filled in the hole. The envelope was buried, but the letter he kept.

Thomas went back home, the letter folded up in his trouser pocket. He would have to hide it somewhere at home until he could figure out exactly what it meant. When he turned into his street he was so deep in thought that he didn't see Eliza coming. He looked up only when he heard her leather leg creaking.

Accidentally, he looked straight into her face and turned as red as a brick.

"Listen, Thomas," said Eliza.

Thomas looked at the tiles of the sidewalk and felt his heart thumping.

"That was ab-so-lute-ly the loveliest letter I have ever received," he heard her say.

So she was not angry. Now he dared look her in the face again. Was she making fun of him?

"I will keep it carefully. And whenever I feel sad, I'll read it."

"Oh," said Thomas. "Good."

"You're such a wonderful boy. Later, when I live in my castle, you can come and visit anytime. We'll go for rides in my Rolls-Royce." She bent over and kissed him on the cheek. Then she walked on.

It was unbelievable! A kiss from Eliza right in the middle of the street. For a letter! His ears were ringing and he heard the music he had heard before, with lots of violins. He jumped for joy. To his amazement, he shot two meters into the air, so light had he become.

At home, he wrote in *The Book of Everything*, "I have to write letters to people. That cheers them up. And then they like me."

He pulled Mrs. van Amersfoort's letter from his pocket. He looked around. Where to hide it? Among the clothes in his cupboard? No, for his mother tidied that up every week. Under the mattress? No. Behind the loose piece of wallpaper? No.

By his side on the table lay *Emil and the Detectives*. He sat staring at it and suddenly he knew. The solution was in the story. A pin. No, he had an even better idea: a safety pin. But how to get hold of a safety pin? Yes! In his head he saw his mother's apron. He crept down the stairs and slipped into the kitchen. There was the apron, hanging on a hook. Not by a loop, but by a safety pin. He took the apron off the hook, snapped open the safety pin, and there, it was his. He hung the apron loosely back over its hook and crept back to his room. He got out the folded letter and worked the safety pin through the four layers of paper. Then he unbuttoned his shirt. With the safety pin he fastened the letter to the inside of his shirt, behind the breast pocket, so you couldn't see it at all from the front. He rebuttoned his shirt. Now he wore Mrs. van Amersfoort's magic spell over his heart.

After the meal, Father read aloud from the Bible:

"And God said to Moses: Pharaoh's heart will still not soften. He will not let the people go. Tomorrow you must go to Pharaoh. He always walks by the water. Wait for him on the bank of the Nile. Take your staff. Strike the water with it, and the water of the Nile will change into blood."

"That is the first plague," Thomas thought. "The water turned as red as cordial. That must have terrified Pharaoh."

"The fishes died and began to stink," Father read on.

"The fishes?" thought Thomas. "The swordtails too? It wasn't the fishes' fault that the Pharaoh was a bad man, was it?"

He looked at his aquarium that stood in the back room, its light glowing. It had a greenish look. Just imagine if the water suddenly turned red as blood ... would that kill the fish? "All the plagues of Egypt," he whispered. "One after the other." He loved his fishes a lot, but sometimes it was necessary to make sacrifices.

"Thus far," said Father, closing the Bible. "What did you say, Thomas?"

"I said, 'All the plagues of Egypt.'"

"Yes," Father said, pleased. "This was the first. Tomorrow we'll do the second."

✻   ✻   ✻

Thomas was playing in the street when a police jeep came around the corner. It stopped, tires squealing, and three policemen jumped out. They ran to number one and rang the bell. At the same time, they kicked the door with their boots. It was quite scary. Very quickly, a lot of people gathered around.

"What's going on?"

"They're picking up Bikkelmans."

"That Nazi?"

"Don't know if he was actually in the Party, but he was as pro-German as . . . eh . . ."

"As Hitler?"

There was laughter. The door opened, and the policemen stormed up the stairs. That's when Mrs. van Amersfoort arrived. She put her heavy shopping bag down and silently watched the stairwell at number one.

"And about time too, eh, Mrs. van Amersfoort?" someone called out.

Mrs. van Amersfoort shrugged and said, "Oh, that little man."

For a long while nothing happened. Then there was thumping and shouting at the top of the stairs. Two policemen came out, a struggling man between them. One pulled the man along by his hair, the other had a tight grip on his neck. The third policeman walked behind the man, pushing him in the back.

"I wish you all had been so brave during the war!" Mrs. van Amersfoort shouted suddenly. "He is a human being, not a pig!"

The policemen took no notice of her. They pushed the man flat down onto the backseat of the jeep. Two of the policemen sat in the front. The third one climbed into the back and sat on top of the man's shoulders. He wrapped his long trench coat around himself so the man became invisible. Only his shouting could be heard over the roar of the engine.

"What sort of manners is that?" Mrs. van Amersfoort yelled. "Haven't you learned anything?" But the jeep tore off, screaming around the corner.

"Did you see that?" Mrs. van Amersfoort shouted angrily.

Nobody answered, so Thomas said, "Yes, I saw that."

People walked away. "Serves him right," someone said. "He was even worse than we thought."

Mrs. van Amersfoort pulled a packet of Golden Fiction cigarettes from her coat pocket and lit one. Then she looked at Thomas. "I should not have shouted like that, Thomas," she said. "But I can't bear to see people treated so roughly. And now I'm completely out of breath."

"Shall I carry your bag in again?" asked Thomas.

"Let's do it together," said Mrs. van Amersfoort. "It's full of books."

She took one handle and Thomas the other one. "What did that man do?" he asked.

"Ah, he belonged to a club that supported the wrong side."

"Oh," said Thomas. "I see."

Mrs. van Amersfoort drank her coffee and Thomas his cordial. One of the cats purred on his lap. It made his legs feel warm.

"I've finished the book," said Thomas.

"And? What did you think of it?"

"Good," said Thomas.

"What did you think was good about it?"

"When all those children helped Emil," said Thomas. "When they caught the villain together. And that business with the pin, that was really good."

Mrs. van Amersfoort nodded.

All you could hear in the silence was the cat's purring.

"I want to ask you something," said Thomas shyly. "It's rather a silly question."

"I've got a silly question too," said Mrs. van Amersfoort. "You go first."

"Can I take the cordial home with me?" asked Thomas. He didn't dare look her in the eyes.

"You can finish it here, can't you?" asked Mrs. van Amersfoort, surprised.

"I mean the bottle," said Thomas. He did not look at her. Of course she was going to ask what for, and he couldn't answer that.

"The bottle . . ." she said. "All right, I can buy a new one."

"Thank you very much," said Thomas. She hadn't asked what for. Maybe she *knew* what for, because she was a witch.

"My turn," said Mrs. van Amersfoort. "A silly question. Here it comes. Thomas, do you ever get hit at home?"

Thomas felt the shock like a punch in his stomach. "Me?!" he blurted. "Of course not!" He thought, "I get a thumping sometimes, but Mama gets hit." "Mama!" he wanted to say. "She's the one who gets hit!" But his throat felt like a tightly screwed-down lid.

For a long while, Mrs. van Amersfoort said nothing. The cat jumped off Thomas's lap and stretched. Thomas quickly emptied his glass. She knew everything, everything. But his mouth was locked. He could not talk. "Jesus . . . Mama . . ." he thought. "What am I going to do?"

"Thank goodness for that," said Mrs. van Amersfoort. "Shall we listen to some music?"

Thomas looked at the clock on the mantelpiece. "It's just about time for me to go home," he said.

"Good," Mrs. van Amersfoort got up. "I'll just pick another book for you. Here, take this one. But I will want it back. *Alone in the World.*"

She saw him to the front door. "I'll lend you this book precisely because you're *not* alone in the world."

"Ah, yes," said Thomas. He looked at her, embarrassed. "And the cordial?" he whispered.

5

"In the name of our Lord Jesus Christ, amen," said Father. He opened his eyes and said, "Good health."

"Good health," said Mother.

"Good health," said Thomas.

"Just look at that!" exclaimed Margot. "The aquarium has gone bright red!"

Father turned around and looked. Mother looked too.

"Good grief," said Thomas. "That's impossible!"

Margot burst out laughing. "I know," she shrieked. But she was laughing so hard she couldn't speak. Tears filled her eyes.

Father got up and went over to the aquarium.

"I know," shouted Margot. "The water has been changed into blood!"

Father came back and sat down. His face was pale. He started eating.

"You'll have to change that water quickly, Thomas," said Mother.

"No, you don't," said Father. "The water stays there."

He took a mouthful and the color slowly returned to his face.

"Hee hee hee," Margot giggled in her dumb way. "It's a miracle."

"In the time of the Pharaoh," said Father, "there were mockers too, who made the water of the Nile change color. Pharaoh's sorcerers. They said, 'Behold, what God can do, we can do too.'"

"But how did they do it?" asked Margot.

"That I don't know," said Father. "But they had been sent by the devil, that much is certain."

"Perhaps there is a germ in the water or something," said Mother nervously.

"I don't think so," said Father. "I think the germ sits at the table here. A human germ who thinks it is amusing to mock God's omnipotence."

"A sorcerer!" Margot shouted enthusiastically.

Thomas looked her in the face and saw something in her eyes he had not seen before. "She's deliberately needling Father," he thought, full of wonder.

"An impostor," said Father. "Like Pharaoh's sorcerers. Men who were possessed by evil."

"Ooh," said Margot. "How exciting, Papa!" She giggled stupidly.

"I'll just change the water in the aquarium later," said Mother.

"No, you will not," said Father. "'*The fishes died and began to stink*,' so it is written."

Mother said no more, and Margot began a story about some book she had to read for school. Nobody listened to her. When everybody had finished eating, Father opened the Bible. He said, "Remember this, Margot. There is only one real book in this world, and that is the Bible. The books you have to read for school have been written by sinful people who are like the Pharaoh's sorcerers. They write books, but they are false books."

"Oh," said Margot. She inspected her fingernails.

"Read them with intelligence and take care that your heart stays with the Bible," said Father.

" '*My heart belongs to Johnny,*' " Margot said softly.

"What did you say?"

"Nothing, Papa."

Father put his glasses on and read aloud: "*But the Egyptian sorcerers did the same through their magic powers: They changed the water into blood. Therefore Pharaoh did not listen to Moses.*

"*Then God said to Moses: 'Go to Pharaoh and say that he must let my people go free. And if he will not do it, tell him that I will afflict all of his territory with frogs. The Nile will teem with frogs and they will penetrate into his house, into his bed, everywhere there will be frogs.'*

"*And so it happened. The frogs covered all of Egypt.*

"*But the sorcerers did the same through their magic powers: They too made frogs appear from everywhere, in all of the land of Egypt.*"

Father closed the Bible and said, "Thus far."

"They were clever, weren't they, those sorcerers," Margot sighed.

"The devil is terribly clever," said Father.

Mother stacked the plates and said, "Here you are, Thomas."

Thomas took the stack of plates out to the kitchen. Mother followed him with the pots and pans. "Get a bucket," she whispered. "Come on."

Thomas followed his mother, carrying the empty bucket. Through the front room, they went to the back room where the aquarium was. Mother slid the cover with the light aside. "Where is the siphon?" she asked.

Thomas put the bucket down. He got a rubber hose from the small cupboard below the aquarium. Mother put one end of the hose into the water and started sucking on the other end.

"What do you think you are doing?" said Father.

They hadn't heard him coming. Mother could not answer with the hose in her mouth. Thomas looked up at his father's face. "Lord Jesus," he thought, "help us!"

Mother pulled the hose out of her mouth and pointed it downward. A jet of red water clattered into the bucket.

"We're changing the water in the aquarium," said Mother.

Father put his hands in his pockets. "What did I say about that?" he asked.

"It has to be done," said Mother, "or the fish will die."

"That will be a good lesson for our wicked sorcerer," said Father.

"I don't think so," said Mother.

"You heard me, woman," said Father. "Stop that immediately."

"No," said Mother.

"Papa," Margot called from the front room. "Can you help me with my geometry?"

"I'm counting to three," said Father.

"Go ahead," said Mother. The red water splashed in the bucket.

"One . . . two . . . three," Father counted.

"Papa," Margot called.

Father jumped forward, yanked the hose out of the aquarium with one hand, and with the other hit Mother in the face. Mother screamed. Then the unbelievable happened: She hit back. She screamed and hit and hit and hit, but only once did she actually strike the man's face. The other blows landed on his arms. Then the man began to punch her wildly, wherever he could. He was much stronger than she was. She crumpled up and fell to the ground weeping. At that moment, it started to rain all over the world.

"Papa!" screamed Margot. "The Bible was written by people. By people!"

Then the front doorbell rang.

The clock went on ticking, but the hands wouldn't move forward. Father listened to the silence, his head angled. Mother sobbed softly. Margot stood next to the table in the front room, stiff and straight as a candle. Thomas tried to stop breathing.

The bell rang again, long and insistently.

"Who could that be?" Father whispered.

"The Lord Jesus," thought Thomas.

Father squatted down next to Mother on the floor. "Upstairs, you," he said. He shook Mother by the shoulder. She scrambled up. Her nose was bleeding. "Here, a handkerchief," said Father. "Quick, upstairs."

Mother stumbled out of the room and up the stairs.

Father went to the top of the stairs that led down to the front door and looked down.

The bell rang again.

He pulled on the rope that hung next to the handrail and the front door clicked open.

Someone stepped inside. "Neighbor?" a woman's voice called. "Could you lend me a cup of sugar?"

Thomas had crept into the hall behind his father. His heart beat wildly, for he had recognized the voice. It was not the Lord Jesus, but Mrs. van Amersfoort.

"Of course, Mrs. van Amersfoort," Father called. "I'll just get it for you."

"Oh, it's you," said Mrs. van Amersfoort. She started climbing the stairs.

"I'll bring it down, just wait there," Father called.

It seemed Mrs. van Amersfoort hadn't understood, for she kept climbing up.

Father hurried into the kitchen, grabbed the sugar, filled up a cup, and rushed back to the stairwell.

But Mrs. van Amersfoort was already there. She stood in the hall holding an empty cup. "What amazing rain all of a sudden," she said.

"Oh," said Father. "You brought your own cup." He poured the sugar into her cup. His hand was shaking.

"Thanks a lot. Isn't your wife here?" asked Mrs. van Amersfoort.

"She's not feeling well," said Father.

"Poor thing. What's wrong with her?"

"A stomach upset," said Father.

Thomas's ears began to ring. He heard the music he had heard before, with lots of violins. "Papa is scared," he thought, full of surprise.

"Perhaps we should have a talk sometime," Mrs. van Amersfoort said.

"A talk?" asked Father.

"Think about it," Mrs. van Amersfoort said. She looked past Father at Thomas. "Hello there, Thomas," she said. "Give your mother a kiss for me."

Slowly, she went down the stairs. "Thanks for the sugar," she called. A moment later, the door slammed shut behind her.

Father fell down on his knees. Sweat dripped from his forehead onto his face. He folded his hands and raised his eyes toward Heaven. "Lord God, forgive me for having let myself go in my anger. What more must I do to bring this household to You? Come to your servant's aid, O Lord. I pray for this in the name of our Lord Jesus Christ, amen."

Thomas looked at the man on the floor. Father had tears in his eyes, but Thomas felt not the slightest pity. "I'm going upstairs," he said. "Should I take the spoon up?"

The man looked at him, his eyes damp. "No, my boy," he said hoarsely. He stretched his arms out toward Thomas. "Come here," he said.

But Thomas took a step back and went up the stairs. When he got to the top, he knocked on his parents' bedroom door. Mother said nothing, but he could hear her sobbing. Gently, he opened the door. She lay prone on the bed, her face turned to the window. He went to her and kissed her wet cheek. He didn't know what to say, so he said nothing.

"Don't do it again, Thomas," she said. "No more plagues of Egypt."

"No, Mama," said Thomas. He waited in case she wanted to say something else, but there was no more.

When he lay in bed, Thomas tried to pray. He had just said, "Lord God, don't forgive him for this, never forgive him . . ." when the Lord Jesus suddenly came on. With His white dress flapping in the breeze, He was standing in the desert or somewhere. There were heaps of sand, anyway, and lots of blue sky.

"Hey there, Thomas," He said. "Everything under control?"

"No," said Thomas.

"What's the matter, then?" asked the Lord.

"Everything," said Thomas. "And, to be honest, You're not being all that much use."

Thomas saw that the Lord was offended, but as it happened, he couldn't care less.

"What do you mean?" asked the Lord Jesus. "What's going on? I have delivered mankind, after all!"

"Delivered?" asked Thomas. "From what exactly, may I ask?"

The Lord frowned. "Oh, come off it. You know perfectly well."

"Blank's my name," said Thomas.

That made the Lord laugh uproariously. You could see He wasn't scared of the dentist. "Okay, okay," said the Lord. "You'll figure that out when you're older."

"Oh, I see," said Thomas.

The Lord Jesus bent over. He wrote in the sand with His finger. When He had finished, He straightened up again. This was written in the sand: *I am pleased that you exist, Thomas!*

The Lord Jesus looked at Thomas and laid His hand on his head. "You are strong, Thomas," He said. "You are strong because you are kind, will you remember that? All of us up here are proud of you. Do you believe that?"

"Yes, Lord Jesus," said Thomas.

"Just call me Jesus," smiled the Lord. "You are after all my favorite boy. I might even call you to me."

He mightn't be all that much use, but it was nice that He came over for a chat now and then. "That would be wonderful, Jesus," said Thomas. Then he fell asleep.

6

"I remember everything," Thomas wrote in *The Book of Everything*. "I forget nothing. I write everything down so that later on I will know exactly what happened."

This is what happened that day: Thomas was woken up by a noise. It was coming from outside. It was as if a thousand people were walking in the street muttering. But that couldn't be, for it was only six o'clock! He got dressed, stood by the window, and looked outside. At first he saw nothing, because his eyes were still asleep, but his ears were awake. The sound was no longer like the sound of people. It was like nothing at all. He looked down and saw that the paving stones had changed color, and so had the tiles of the sidewalks. They were kind of greenish. Once his eyes had woken up properly, he saw that everything was moving. The street and the sidewalks were covered in something greenish that moved. Suddenly he knew: frogs! Brueghel Street was covered in frogs. When he looked across toward Apollo Avenue, he could see no end to the stream of frogs. When he looked at Jan van Eyck Street, he saw them streaming in from that direction too. They were croaking. The sound was like that of the rubbish collector's rattle, only this sounded like a thousand rattles at once. He opened the window and looked straight down. He saw that the frogs were gathering in front of the door. They climbed on one another's backs and stacked themselves up. He could not see the door, but he saw that the frogs were stacked up high against the wall of his house. He had never seen such an enormous stack of frogs before. Were they trying to force the door open with their weight? "Mama," he thought anxiously. "I didn't do this. Blank's my name."

He crept out of his room and tiptoed down the stairs. He looked at the front door down below. There was a thrumming as if a million fingers were tapping on it. He thought, "Any moment now the door is going to cave in." He did not know what to do.

Slowly he went down the stairs. Halfway down, there was a smell of ditch water. The front door rattled in its frame. It was frightening. He turned and ran back upstairs. "Mama will have to believe me," he thought. "But of course she won't. And Papa won't either." He sat down on the floor at the top of the stairs. He was in despair. If a trillion frogs wanted to get inside the house, it was pretty obviously his fault. Who else's fault could it be? He was trapped. His mother wanted no more plagues of Egypt, because they caused too much trouble. His father thought he was mocking God. He was in a real fix. How would Remi in *Alone in the World* deal with it? Suddenly he knew. He had to go and talk to the frogs.

He started down the stairs again, but when he smelled the ditch water he thought, "How do you talk to frogs?"

He answered his own question. "Well, just like people, of course. Remi talks to his animals all the time. Frogs aren't stupid, you know."

When he got downstairs, he put his hand against the door. He felt it shaking and heard it groan under the weight of the frogs. "They're friendly frogs," he thought. "They've come to help Mama and me. It is well meant, but God has hardened Pharaoh's heart."

He knelt and tried to push open the letterbox. That was not so easy, for it was jammed tight with frogs. He pushed and pushed until he managed to open the letterbox just a bit. Immediately, ten frog legs poked through the chink, as if he were in a horror story. But he didn't like horror stories, so that couldn't be. His Granddad had *Grimm's Fairy Tales*. Thomas always skipped the one called "The Youth Who Wanted to Learn What Fear Was." He thought it was spooky enough at Granddad's, because Granddad took his teeth out of his mouth while Thomas was watching. Scary! But Granddad was okay. He did believe in God, but not too badly. He never hit anyone. When he was angry, he shouted, "The spider broom! The spider broom!" but Thomas had no idea why.

"Hello," he said softly through the letterbox.

He didn't want to wake Father and Mother.

"Hello, I'm Thomas."

For a moment it seemed that not a single frog had heard him. The legs kept wriggling and the croaking rattled on. But the noise gradually became softer and sounded farther and farther away. The frogs in the front ranks had fallen silent.

"Dear frogs," he said. "Thanks very much for coming. But you can't come inside here, because my mother won't allow it. And *What Mother Says, Goes*. Have you heard of that? It is a radio program for when I have school sickness. So please return to your ditches and canals. Thank you all for services rendered." Thomas loved words, particularly if he didn't understand them.

It became quiet far and near. Then the rattling started again, at first near the door, then farther and farther away. It sounded excited, and Thomas worried that they might not have understood him. But then the frog legs withdrew from the letterbox. The croaking grew softer. It sounded like people muttering. It became more and more quiet. He waited and waited. The door stopped shaking, the drumming ceased. He pushed open the letterbox and had a look. The frogs were withdrawing!

"Thomas!" called Margot. "Thomas, what are you doing there?"

He looked up. Margot stood at the top of the stairs in her nightdress.

"Ssshhh," he hissed. He ran up the stairs without making a sound.

"What were you doing there?" asked Margot.

"There were frogs," said Thomas. "But Mama doesn't want this."

"What doesn't Mama want?"

"The plagues of Egypt."

Margot looked at him for a long moment. "Thomas," she said then.

"Yes?"

"How many frogs were there?"

"Millions."

"True? Did you see them yourself?"

"With my own eyes."

Margot slowly shook her head. "Thomas," she said. "You mustn't always believe your eyes."

Thomas shrugged.

"You must keep your head," said Margot. "Don't let yourself be driven mad."

"No," said Thomas.

"Thomas?"

"Yes?"

"You know what Eliza said to me the other day?"

Thomas blushed. He shook his head.

"'What a nice brother you've got,' she said."

"Oh," said Thomas.

He looked at the coat hooks on the wall. The overcoats were busy hanging.

"You know what, Thomas?" said Margot. "Eliza is right."

Thomas quickly examined her face. Perhaps Margot was not as stupid as he had always thought.

They sat together at the top of the stairs. Thomas couldn't remember them ever sitting on the stairs together before. It was a special feeling.

"Do you know what 'dishonors' means?" Thomas asked.

Margot looked at him. "Dishonors? 'Dishonors' means you lose your honor. For example, ah . . . I can't think of an example."

"Doesn't matter," said Thomas. "But what is 'honor'?"

"Wait," said Margot. "I've got it. 'Dishonors' means you lose your dignity."

Thomas sighed. What was "dignity"?

He moved his hand inside his shirt and undid the safety pin. He pulled Mrs. van Amersfoort's folded-up letter from under his shirt and read, "*A man who hits his wife dishonors himself.*"

"Show me," said Margot. She read the line for herself. "Who did you get this from? This is just sooo true!"

"Can't tell," said Thomas. "It's a secret."

Margot cocked her head and listened to the silence. "Papa must read this," she whispered.

"And if he gets angry?" asked Thomas.

"He must," said Margot. She handed the letter back to Thomas. "He really must."

"Not yet," said Thomas. He pinned the letter back under his shirt.

"Ah, yes," said Father that evening as he cut the meat. "I nearly forgot. This morning when I went out of the front door, there was a frog sitting in the corner of the porch. The poor little thing was so scared, it had clapped its little hands over its eyes."

Margot choked on her endive. Mother glanced at Thomas, but Thomas pretended not to notice. Her nose was red and swollen. There was a small piece of cotton wool in her nostril.

"I had a strange experience too," said Margot when she'd stopped coughing. "I was sent out of Dutch class."

"What?" Father said, shocked. "This can't be true."

"It is, though," said Margot. "Mr. de Rijp said I was a smart aleck and then I had to get out."

"What's a 'smart aleck'?" asked Thomas.

"Someone who thinks he always knows better about everything," Father explained. "And that is very annoying."

"I know something better," thought Thomas. "What if my parents gave me away to an old musician called Vitalis, like in *Alone in the World*. He would have dogs and a monkey with a difficult name. And the old musician would die on our travels and then I would be alone in the world. With Eliza."

"But what did you actually say?" Father asked Margot. You could see he was worried.

"I said I didn't want to read those false books for my list," said Margot. "I said that the Bible was enough for me."

It became so terribly quiet that Thomas woke out of his thoughts. He saw that Father had gone red in the face. "Jesus!" he thought, but the Lord did not show up.

"Now you listen to me, Margot," Father said nervously. "You haven't understood at all. The books you have to read contain the opinions of people. In the Bible, there are not opinions, but truths. Because the Bible is God's word. That is what I meant. That doesn't mean you can go and be insolent to your teacher!"

"I only said what I've learnt from you," said Margot virtuously. She chewed her meat enthusiastically. "Nice meal, Mama."

Mother glanced at her and smiled.

"So tomorrow," Father said loudly. "Tomorrow . . ." His voice cracked. "Tomorrow you will go and see Mr. de Rijp and apologize."

"Okay, Papa," said Margot. She did not look at her father. "Shall I do your hair later, Mama?"

"What is this world coming to?" Father exclaimed. "I just can't believe it. You will read all the books that are assigned, understood?"

"Yes, Papa," said Margot. "Shall I plait it for you, Mama?"

"That would be nice, Margot," said Mother.

"Do you know *Alone in the World*?" Thomas asked Father. "It's about a boy who is all alone in the world."

But Father didn't hear. He angrily mashed his potatoes with his fork.

"That book is sad," said Thomas. "But it is exciting too."

He felt Mother's hand on his head. "Eat up, Thomas," she said.

When Mother said that, he knew he'd better keep his mouth shut for a while.

"Why don't you say something?" Father said. "She is your daughter too, you know."

Mother looked at him. "Ah," she said. "You say all that so much better than I could."

An icy silence followed.

"Smart aleck," Thomas thought. "Good word. Must remember it."

"So where did you get that book from?" Father asked suddenly.

"Book?" said Thomas.

"*Alone in the World*," said Father impatiently.

Thomas felt rigid with fear.

"From me," Margot said casually.

Thomas looked at her, speechless.

"Oh," said Father. He looked distrustful. "And how did you get hold of it?"

"A Saint Nicholas Day present years ago," said Margot.

Father bent over his plate.

"He's eating," thought Thomas, relieved.

Father read about the third plague of Egypt: all the world's dust changed into gnats. Everyone was bitten viciously. The whole world was itching. But Thomas knew Mother did not want it, so a plague like that was no use to him. A different plan was needed to change Pharaoh's heart. But Thomas could not think of any plan.

Father closed the Bible. "Let us pray," he said. He folded his hands and closed his eyes. "Lord our God . . ."

"Listen to this, Thomas," Thomas heard. It was the Lord Jesus. He stood calling in the wilderness. "I haven't had an easy time with my father either, you know."

"Really?" asked Thomas.

"Really," said the Lord. "He was very strict. I had to be nailed to the Cross whether I wanted to or not."

"Oh yes," said Thomas. "That wasn't very nice for you."

"No," said the Lord. "It happened once, but never again. And now I've lost Him on top of it all."

"Who?" asked Thomas.

"God the Father," said the Lord Jesus. "I can't find Him anywhere. Searched all over Heaven. Very strange. He disappeared after your last beating. I think it got to be too much for Him."

"You think?" Thomas asked.

"I think He loved you very much, Thomas, and that He couldn't bear it anymore. That is my personal opinion."

"In the name of our Lord Jesus Christ, amen," said Father.

"Bye, Jesus," Thomas whispered. And then the doorbell rang.

7

Aunt Pie came storming up the stairs. Thomas stood at the top of the stairs waiting for her. It was as if the sun was rolling into the house. With Aunt Pie, warmth streamed into the cold hallway.

"Hello, my boy," said Aunt Pie. She was wearing a large hat fastened with a hatpin. She kissed Thomas from underneath her hat.

"Hello, Aunt Pie," said Thomas.

He always liked it when Aunt Pie came. But this time was different. Aunt Pie did not look happy. Her face was covered in red spots.

"You're such a gorgeous boy," she said. Her voice sounded hoarse, as if she had been crying. She walked on and sailed into the living room with her flapping hat. She went up to the table, planted her hands on her hips, and called, "Benno has hit me!"

The earth trembled and Heaven held its breath. The birds in the trees fell silent and the wind died down. Church bells started ringing of their own accord and trams ground to a halt. Uncle Benno had hit Aunt Pie! Bewilderment spread through the land.

"And do you know why?" shouted Aunt Pie. "Because I bought a pair of slacks! He hit me because I was wearing trousers! Has he gone completely off his head?"

Mother, Margot, Thomas, and Father stared at Aunt Pie as if she were a ghost. Father had gone pale. Then he said, "Margot and Thomas, go to your room. Aunt Pie and I have something to discuss."

"No, not at all!" said Aunt Pie. "There's nothing secret about it." She looked from Margot to Thomas and back again. "Margot, Thomas, your Uncle Benno has hit your Aunt Pie. There."

"Have a seat, Pie," said Mother. She got up and pulled over a chair. Aunt Pie sat down.

"And I think that you"— Aunt Pie stabbed her finger at Father — "that you, as his eldest brother, need to go and talk with him. You have to tell him that he just cannot do this. If not, I am going to stand in front of our house with a placard that says 'Mr. Klopper Beats His Wife Because She Wears Trousers.' So there. Has he gone totally bonkers?"

"Calm down, Pie," said Father with a trembling voice. "It is simply a fact of life that the man is the head of the household . . ."

"But that doesn't mean he has to go about belting everybody!" exclaimed Aunt Pie.

"Listen, Pie," Father said severely. "Let me finish. It is the man's task to lead and instruct his wife and children. And if they refuse to listen to him, he has no choice but to . . ."

"Beat?" screamed Aunt Pie.

". . . but to take severe measures. That is how God has ordained things. God has also ordained that women wear dresses and men, trousers."

Aunt Pie grinned maliciously. "Ludicrous!" she shouted.

Father raised his voice. "And if you obstinately resist God's commandments, your husband has the right, no, the duty, to compel you to obey, with a hard hand if need be."

Aunt Pie regarded Father mockingly. "Oh, is that so?" she said sweetly. She opened her handbag and produced a packet of cigarettes. She drew one out and lit it, then blew a cloud of smoke at the light. "Okay," she said. "You are obviously useless. But I tell you this: If Benno hits me just once more, I'm off, and he'll never see me again. And from now on, all I'll wear is trousers. Look."

She lifted one leg above the table. It was covered by a pink trouser leg. She winked at Thomas. "Don't you agree, my sweet?"

Thomas quickly glanced at Father. "Blank's my name," he thought.

"What's happened to your nose, anyway?" Aunt Pie asked Mother. "You haven't been resisting God's commandments, I hope?"

"No, nothing," Mother said awkwardly. She looked at the tablecloth. There were a few gravy stains on it.

"Only joking," said Aunt Pie. "So how come your nose is so swollen?"

"Oh, nothing," said Mother. "I bumped into something."

"Into the aquarium," said Margot. "Didn't she, Papa?"

Thomas felt the fear in his stomach. "Don't, Margot," he thought. "Don't needle."

Aunt Pie puffed small clouds of smoke up at the ceiling. "Yes," she said. "They can do nasty things to you, those aquariums. I'm forever bumping into aquariums, usually with my nose."

"Shall I make some coffee?" said Mother nervously.

"Not for me," said Aunt Pie. She looked at Father venomously. "I have suddenly realized something," she said. "You're just as big a coward as your brother."

"Pie," said Mother. "You're mistaken. . . ."

Aunt Pie squashed her cigarette on Father's plate. "Duty calls," she said. "Back to my pious husband with the flapping hands. But I'll teach him! You just watch me!"

She bent and kissed Mother, then Margot, and finally Thomas. "We're not going to take things lying down, are we?" she said. Then she sailed out of the room with her hat and floated down the stairs.

Silence descended. No one dared look at anyone. Thomas

could smell Aunt Pie. Her smoke and her perfume still hung under the light.

"Isn't it time you did your homework, Margot?" Father asked. His voice sounded like an empty bucket.

"Yes, Papa, but first I'll do Mama's hair."

"Oh," said Father. He got up. "I've got things to do for work," he said. He withdrew into the side room, where his desk stood.

"How did you like those frogs?" asked Mrs. van Amersfoort.

Thomas was surprised. He was sitting in the chair with the carved legs. A black cat was rubbing against his legs.

"Quite good," he said. "But Mama doesn't want this."

"I can imagine," said Mrs. van Amersfoort. "It was rather meant to be a joke. I think it's actually not a very practical plague."

Thomas took a gulp of his cordial to recover from the shock. Mrs. van Amersfoort was a powerful witch. Much more powerful even than he had thought.

"Listen to this," she said. "This is fun." A small book lay in her lap. "You've got an aquarium, haven't you?"

Thomas nodded. Mrs. van Amersfoort knew everything.

"Listen," she said. She put her glasses on and read aloud.

Master Sweet
washed his feet
on Saturdays in the aquarium.
And as he splashed
and as he splattered
he warbled: "Hum-tiddly-um-tum!"

When she had finished, she gave Thomas a questioning glance. "Well, what do you think?"

"Funny," said Thomas seriously.

"I think she's such a wonderful writer, Annie M. G. Schmidt," said Mrs. van Amersfoort. "She writes for the newspaper."

"Oh," said Thomas. "But what does that poem mean?"

"Nothing, really," said Mrs. van Amersfoort. "It's just fun."

"Ah, yes," said Thomas. He considered. It was just fun.

"Music usually means nothing much either," said Mrs. van Amersfoort. "It is just beautiful."

"Yes, yes," he said. "Just beautiful. Now I see."

"The forest and the sea don't mean anything either, do they," said Mrs. van Amersfoort. "Forest is forest and sea is sea. You can enjoy them."

"Yes, yes," said Thomas. "Enjoy." He thought about the beach and the sea. About building sand castles against the tide.

Of catching shrimps in a net. "We go to Zandvoort for the day sometimes," he said.

"And how do you like that?"

"Great," Thomas sighed.

"And what does Zandvoort mean?" she asked.

Thomas laughed. He had understood. "Nothing," he said. "It's just great."

The cat jumped onto his lap. It was warm and soft. He could feel the purring right through his body. It was just good to be at Mrs. van Amersfoort's place, even though her husband had been shot dead with guns.

"Will you do something for me?" she asked.

"Of course," said Thomas.

"Will you read to me? Here." Mrs. van Amersfoort put the book by Annie M. G. Schmidt down on top of the cat in his lap. "Start at the beginning."

Thomas felt himself blush. At school, he often had to read aloud, but he had never done it in someone's home. It was a strange feeling. He opened the book and began.

At first, he stumbled over some of the words. But it quickly became easier. At times, Mrs. van Amersfoort laughed. He didn't know why. He was too busy reading.

It was miraculous. Weren't these supposed to be children's rhymes? So why did they make a grown-up person laugh? He raised his eyes from his book occasionally so he could see her face. When she laughed, funny wrinkles darted from her mouth to her ears. Her head nodded as if she were saying, "Yes! Yes! Yes!" And without him noticing, she had grown two plaits, bows and all.

At first, Thomas didn't know what he was seeing, but that didn't last long. He saw that Mrs. van Amersfoort was not an old lady, but an old little girl. She might jump out of her chair any moment and grab her jump rope. That's what she looked like.

Thomas read and read. Mrs. van Amersfoort was a witch, but now she was under a spell herself. That was a good feeling. Thomas wanted never to stop reading aloud, never.

"That was lovely," said Mrs. van Amersfoort when Thomas had read five poems. "But now I need a rest. You know, my husband used to read aloud to me. We always enjoyed that so much." The plaits had gone, and so had the bows. Her gray bun was back.

"I think I shall start a reading-aloud club," said Thomas.

"What a good idea," said Mrs. van Amersfoort.

"With music in the breaks," said Thomas. "We'll need a program, otherwise people won't know what to expect. For instance:

"Item one: Psalm 22, recited by Thomas Klopper, because I already know that one by heart.

"Item two: Music from Mrs. van Amersfoort's portable gramophone.

"Item three: *Emil and the Detectives*, chapter one, read by Thomas Klopper.

"Item four: Music from Mrs. van Amersfoort's portable gramophone.

"Item five . . ."

"Very good, excellent," said Mrs. van Amersfoort. "How come you know that psalm by heart?"

"We have to know a psalm by heart every Monday for school," said Thomas.

"How about saying it for me?" said Mrs. van Amersfoort.

"Okay," said Thomas.

He gently pushed the cat from his lap, stood up, and said:

(WARNING: You can safely skip the poem Thomas is about to recite. It is totally unreadable!)

> *My God, my God, oh why have you abandoned me, oh why?*
> *And why do you forsake me while in grief I groan and cry*
> *And struggle 'gainst the bitter blows the evil fiend still sends.*
> *And if I pray at daybreak or implore you when day ends,*
> *My pleas remain unheard, your silence puts me to the test:*
> *I suffer still and from my tribulations find no rest.*

"Goodness gracious," exclaimed Mrs. van Amersfoort when Thomas had finished. "Very clever. And so cheerful for children, don't you think?"

Thomas sat down. "Eh . . . yes," he said. "But it is very difficult to learn by heart, you know."

"I could never do it," said Mrs. van Amersfoort. "Good, so now you have a reading-aloud club and a program. And where are you going to do it?"

"What do you mean, where?" said Thomas, surprised.

"Well," said Mrs. van Amersfoort. "A club needs a meeting place. Where is the meeting place?"

Thomas suddenly felt embarrassed. He knew where, but he didn't dare say it.

"I know what we'll do," said Mrs. van Amersfoort. "We'll do it here, but the program will have to be changed a little. You read poems by Annie M. G. Schmidt, and I take care of the audience."

"Good," said Thomas.

"Take the book home with you," said Mrs. van Amersfoort. "So you can practice."

Thomas went home and practiced till he was cross-eyed.

t was a windy day with a lot of rain. A day that would shake the world. For ever after, trams would scream as they rounded a corner. Men walked through the streets with grim faces, not liking one another.

"It seemed like an ordinary day," Thomas wrote in *The Book of Everything*. "But that was because I hadn't paid proper attention. I should have known, because my ears were already ringing when I woke up. My window was rattling, so I couldn't think. And I couldn't find my socks."

But good things had happened too on that day. When Thomas was walking home from school, he saw Eliza coming out of Mrs. van Amersfoort's house. That surprised him. He had never seen Eliza there before.

She came up to him, *creak, creak,* and spread her arms. "Come here, my favorite friend," she said. She embraced him and pressed him firmly against her chest. That was nice, for it felt as if his head lay on a bouncy pillow. He looked up into her face. Eliza had put lipstick on. When she smiled at him, he thought he would expire on the spot. "And I wouldn't have minded at all," he wrote in *The Book of Everything*. "Luckily she held me for a long while and I thought, 'Girls are nice.' I will never forget that, because I never forget anything. I write everything down. This too: 'Perhaps Eliza cannot find a boyfriend because she has a leather leg and a bad hand. Perhaps she is waiting for me to grow up a bit. My good fortune.'"

"Mrs. van Amersfoort tells me you're very good at reading aloud," said Eliza. "I'm looking forward to it."

Then she let go of Thomas. She left a terrible emptiness. "I'll wait for you forever," Thomas whispered. But once she turned the corner, he waited no longer. His ears buzzed. He rang the bell and Mother opened the door.

"Hello, Mama," he said.

"Hello, my dream prince," said Mother. Her nose had healed quite well. The cotton wool was gone. He wasn't a dream prince, really, he was more of a thinker. But Mother meant well.

"Mrs. van Amersfoort tells me you've started a reading-aloud club," she said. "That should be fun."

It seemed the whole world knew about it.

"Yes," said Thomas. "But I have to practice." He ran up the stairs to his room.

"Don't you want a drink?" Mother called.

"No, rather not," he responded, closing the door.

But he did not practice. He sat in front of the window to think. The window rattled in the wind, so the thinking was rather jerky. He thought, "I am a coward, because I'm scared."

Then he thought nothing for a while. He listened to the window rattling.

"I don't like cowards," he thought next. "But that is how I am."

Every day, he had pinned Mrs. van Amersfoort's letter to his clean shirt. Now he undid his shirt and unpinned the letter. He folded it open, read it, and sighed deeply. The world held its breath. Would Thomas do it? Would Thomas dare? The world did not know. The world was waiting in suspense.

"Let this cut of suffering be taken away from me," he thought. Thomas did not know what those words meant, but he knew Jesus had said them when He knew He was going to die. They were beautiful words that brought tears to Thomas's eyes.

"Don't be afraid," he thought.

He stood up with the letter in his hand. He crept down the stairs.

When they had finished eating, Father opened the Bible. Thomas's throat felt like a screw-top lid.

"What is this?" Father asked. A sheet of paper lay in the Bible, right on top of the plagues of Egypt.

Father read it. Then he turned the letter over, but the other side was blank. "So," he said. He had turned pale.

No one said anything, but Margot hummed a hit tune.

"Good," said Father. "I'll read it to you." He cleared his throat. He seemed calm, but his fingers trembled.

"'*A man who hits his wife dishonors himself,*'" he read. He put the letter down next to the Bible and smoothed it out. "I agree with that completely," he said. "But there is something missing. It should read, 'A man who hits his wife *without good reason* dishonors himself.'"

"Tiddlyum, tiddlyum, tiddlyum-tum-tum," hummed Margot.

"Would you mind turning off that music, Margot?" Father asked.

"Of course, Papa. Sorry," said Margot.

"All right," said Father. "The letter itself doesn't matter a great deal. The important question is why it is in the Bible and who put it there. It would seem that someone is out to turn us against each other. Someone who wants to draw our family away from God and His institutions. Entirely in the spirit of these times, of course."

Father looked first at Mother, then at Margot, then at Thomas. "So the question is, who put this letter in the Bible?" He took it between his thumb and index finger and waved it about.

It was as if all life on earth had died out, it was so still. It woke the dead in the churchyards. They pricked up their ears, but heard nothing.

"No one?" asked Father. He tapped his fingers on the table. "Someone at this table is lying. I do not know who it is, but nothing remains hidden from God's eye. Let us ask Him for help."

He folded his hands on top of the Bible and closed his eyes.

"Almighty God," he said. "See our plight. Help this family to be strong in this time of great temptation. . . ."

Thomas closed his eyes. The sky turned clear blue and sand blew around his ears. "Jesus?" he asked. But Jesus was nowhere to be seen.

"I'm here," said Jesus.

"Where?" said Thomas. "I can't see you."

"That's pretty obvious," said Jesus. "You've got your eyes shut."

Thomas opened his eyes. Jesus stood in the room, in front of the chimney-piece with the copper geckoes. He looked at the praying man.

"So that's him?" asked Jesus.

"Yes," said Thomas.

"He means well, I think," said Jesus. "But he is afraid. He is really a coward, if you ask me."

"I don't know," said Thomas.

"He hides like a scared child behind God's broad back," said Jesus.

But Thomas thought, "How can you hide behind the back of someone who is no longer there?"

"I have to tell you something," he said.

"Go on then," said Jesus.

"God the Father is not just not here," said Thomas. "He has died. I'm telling You honestly."

Jesus was stunned, and for a moment He was speechless. "You really mean it!" he exclaimed.

Thomas nodded. He thought it was sad for the Lord Jesus, but the truth had to be stated.

"But how did this happen?" Jesus cried.

"He was beaten out of me," said Thomas. "And then He died, for He could not do without me."

Jesus had to think about that. Then He nodded and smiled sadly. Of course, that was how it had been. Without Thomas, nothing could exist.

"We pray for this in the name of our Lord Jesus Christ, amen," Father said.

Jesus waved to Thomas and faded. Thomas waved back.

"What are you doing?" Father asked.

"I was waving," said Thomas.

"What for?"

"I saw Jesus," said Thomas.

Margot giggled and Mother laid her arm on Thomas's shoulder in fear.

Father flushed. He hit the Bible hard with the flat of his hand, making the dust of three thousand years swirl. "I will not put up with this," he shouted, red in the face. "In my house, there will be no jokes about our Lord and Redeemer. Is that understood?"

Thomas bent his head. He hadn't been joking. He didn't feel the slightest bit like joking.

"Is that understood?" Father repeated.

"Yes, Papa," said Thomas.

"And now I want to know who put that letter into the Bible."

"I did," said Margot.

Everyone stared at Margot, but she did not stare back. "Tiddlyum, tiddlyum," she hummed.

Father shook his head. "I don't believe a word of it," he said.

Margot shrugged.

"Who wrote it?" Father asked. "I don't recognize the handwriting."

"Found it in the street," said Margot. "Tiddlyum, tiddlyum-tum-tum-tum."

"You're lying," said Father. "We all know who has done this." He looked around the circle.

Thomas's heart missed a beat when he felt his father's eyes on him. It lasted only a moment. Father looked at Mother. "Don't we?" he said.

"Yes," said Mother. "I did it."

Thomas looked at her, horrified, and felt himself grow angry inside—so angry that his fear burst apart into a thousand pieces. "Not true!" he screamed. "It was me who did it! Me!"

Father looked at him severely. "You are a liar, Thomas," he said.

"But—" shouted Thomas.

"Silence!" Father thundered.

"I did it! Me, I did it!" Thomas was weeping with fury. "There are pinholes in that letter. Pinholes! And do you know how they got there? I made them with a safety pin. This one." He rummaged in his trouser pocket and tossed the safety pin on the table.

Father, Mother, and Margot stared at the pin as if their lives depended on it. It glinted in the lamplight. "I could actually hear the safety pin," Thomas wrote in *The Book of Everything*. "It made a high-pitched sound, like someone screaming in the distance."

Father stretched the letter between his hands and held it up. The paper was bright in the glow of the lamp.

"It is true," Father muttered. "There are pinholes in it." He lowered the paper. "You were not lying, Thomas. I falsely accused you. Forgive me. But more important is that someone has used you, Thomas. Someone is trying to turn you against your father. Who is that, Thomas? Who wrote this letter?"

"That is a secret," said Thomas.

"Aunt Pie?"

"It is a secret," said Thomas.

"Thomas," said Father.

"Yes?"

"Tell me who wrote this letter."

"No, Papa."

"Thomas, fetch the spoon, go upstairs, and wait for me."

A hot wind came up, scorching the earth. The trees shriveled up and the animals fled. Everything was desolate and empty. No one could live on the earth any longer.

"Except perhaps the gnats," thought Thomas. "And bubonic plague."

"No," said Mother quietly. "Thomas stays where he is and you read from the Bible."

Father glared at her furiously.

"I'll get the spoon, Mama," said Thomas.

Mother took his hand. "No," she said. "My brave hero stays here sitting next to me."

"Tiddlyum, tiddlyam," sang Margot. "How happy I am."

Thomas was frightened by the cold look in her eyes.

"Woman!" said Father. "Do not contradict me!"

"Mama," said Thomas. "It's all right, just let me go."

"No," said Mother. "You have not deserved any punishment." She kept a firm hold on his hand.

"Tiddlydum, tiddlydim, I find no guilt in him," Margot sang.

Father stood up. His head rose like a balloon, higher and higher. The ceiling came down and the room became smaller and smaller. "Woman!" he thundered. "Let go of that child."

Mother got up too, pulling Thomas along with her. "No," she said. Her chair tottered.

Father walked around the table, gripped Thomas by his other arm, and tugged.

"No!" screamed Mother.

Father raised his hand at her threateningly.

No one had been minding Margot. Suddenly, she was there, as if she came falling from the sky. In her right hand, the carving knife flashed, and her eyes blazed. She jumped in front of her father and pointed the knife at his throat. Father let go of Thomas and stared at the knife.

"She looked like an angel," wrote Thomas in *The Book of Everything*. "The most dangerous angel in Heaven. One of those with a flaming sword."

"Hands off," Margot snarled. "I've had enough of this. I've had it up to here." She brushed the knife along her throat.

"Don't, Margot," Mother whispered. "Put that knife away."

But Margot wasn't listening. "Goddamn it," she said.

The curse was worse than the knife. It cut through the soul.

"Mama and Thomas have no reason to be afraid of God," she hissed. "Because they are kind. You are not kind." She made a stabbing movement with the knife. "Don't think I won't dare," she growled. "I am like you. I am not kind either."

Father collapsed like a dying elephant and finished up on his knees. "This family is doomed," he groaned. "The spirit of the time has poisoned you. Let us pray."

And he started praying loudly.

"I don't give a damn what you believe," Margot shouted. "But there will be no more hitting."

The man was startled out of his prayer and looked at her wildly.

"You know that it is wrong," Margot said coldly. "But you do it anyway." She took a deep breath. "As long as the neighbors don't notice. As long as the family doesn't notice. As long as nobody in the office finds out! Isn't it true?"

The man got up turned furiously, and stalked to the door. He stopped and looked back into the room with his red eyes. "I cannot stay under the same roof as you," he roared. "I AM GOING TO SLEEP IN A HOTEL."

He yanked the door open and disappeared into the hallway. Then he rumbled down the stairs. The front door slammed shut like a clap of thunder.

"Tiddlyum, tiddlyum-tum-tum," Margot hummed. She put the carving knife back on the table and sat down. She planted her elbows on the table and covered her face with her hands. Mother and Thomas stayed where they stood.

Two sparrows played their piercing trumpets on the windowsill.

"Child, what have you done?" Mother whispered.

Margot lowered her hands. Her face was as white as a sheet. Her eyes showed nothing at all. "I've put a stop to it," she said. Then she burst into tears.

Mother sat down, shaking her head disconsolately. "You threatened your father with a knife," she said. "What is to become of us?"

Margot glared at her. "Would you prefer to be beaten up?" she sobbed. She jumped up. "Oh, yes. I nearly forgot." She ran into the kitchen and came back with the wooden spoon. She rested one end of it on the threshold of the living room door and stamped it in half. "Out with it," she said. She took the two pieces and opened the window. The sparrows flew up trumpeting.

"Not from the window," said Mother.

But already the spoon was sailing through the air in two pieces.

Thomas went across to Margot. She took him in her arms and held him tight.

Father stayed out for an hour. Then he came back home. He crept up the stairs like a cat and withdrew into the side room. He said he had work to do.

9

There had been a change of plans. Thomas didn't know why. The first meeting of the reading-aloud club was not to be held at Mrs. van Amersfoort's.

"We're going to have it at your house," she said.

It gave Thomas a bit of a shock. "But why?" he asked anxiously.

"We thought it would be nice," said Mrs. van Amersfoort. "Me, your mother, and your Aunt Pie."

Mama? Aunt Pie? What was going on?

Suddenly, Thomas didn't think it was fun anymore. His house was not a house where he could bring his friends. And it was absolutely not a house for a reading-aloud club.

"And we're not doing it in the afternoon," said Mrs. van Amersfoort. "We're going to start at seven o'clock in the evening."

Thomas didn't want his cordial anymore. He put the glass down among the books on the table. "I felt worried in my stomach," he wrote in *The Book of Everything*. "As if I had swallowed a rhinoceros."

"And . . . when?" he asked. His voice squeaked like a bicycle wheel.

"You'll be surprised," said Mrs. van Amersfoort. She looked at him mischievously over her steaming cup of coffee. "Shall I tell you?"

Thomas nodded.

"Tonight," said Mrs. van Amersfoort.

Thomas stared at her vacantly. "Papa is not going to allow that," he thought but didn't say.

"Don't worry, Thomas," said Mrs. van Amersfoort. "You must not be afraid. You wanted the plagues of Egypt, didn't you? Not the frogs, not the gnats and not the bubonic plague, but we are the best plague, we women and children. No Pharaoh can resist us."

"Oh," said Thomas. "I see." Fear crept into his throat like a frog.

"Shut your eyes, Thomas," said Mrs. van Amersfoort.

For a moment he didn't understand what she said. "Shut my eyes? Oh, yes, shut my eyes." He did as she said.

"Breathe slowly and put your hands in your lap."

Thomas's ears began to ring, and a moment later he heard music he had heard before, with lots of violins.

"What can you see now?"

"Nothing," said Thomas. "Or . . . wait a moment. Yes, yes, there it is. I can see a desert."

"And what do you see in that desert?"

"Sand," said Thomas.

"Nothing else?"

"Yes," said Thomas. "But I won't tell you, for you'll think I'm making fun of you."

"I don't think so," said Mrs. van Amersfoort. "Go ahead and tell me."

"I see Jesus," said Thomas. "Do you think that's awful?"

"Not a bit," said Mrs. van Amersfoort. "I've faced worse things."

"There is something strange about Him," Thomas muttered. "Hang on. Now I can see what it is. His beard is gone! But there is something else . . . Let me have another look." Thomas frowned. "Oh no, I'm not telling you this. This is really impossible." He shook his head. He didn't dare say that Jesus looked very like his mother when she had her hair down, for no one would understand.

There was a silence, singing like a safety pin.

Then Mrs. van Amersfoort said, "Oh."

"He always talks to me," Thomas told her.

"Gosh," said Mrs. van Amersfoort. "Do you like that? Because we can just get rid of Him otherwise."

"I don't mind," said Thomas. "He is all alone, you know. I think He has no one else to talk to."

"Oh, that's terribly sad," said Mrs. van Amersfoort. "What is He saying now?"

"He says He is coming tonight," said Thomas.

"The more the merrier," said Mrs. van Amersfoort. "Thomas? You can open your eyes now."

Thomas looked at her. The rhinoceros in his stomach had disappeared and so had the frog in his throat.

"Are you still scared?" Mrs. van Amersfoort asked.

"No," said Thomas.

He heard a rustling above his head. It was the angels clapping.

After the meal, Father read from the Bible. And these were the last sentences. "*Moses said: Tonight, God will go out into the midst of Egypt. All the eldest sons of the Egyptians will die. Pharaoh's eldest son, the Crown Prince, as well as the eldest son of the maidservant and also the first-born of all the beasts. And there shall be a loud cry throughout the land of Egypt, such as there has never been before nor ever will be again.*"

"Why did all these sons have to die?" Thomas asked. "Why not Pharaoh himself?" Father opened his mouth to answer, but Mother jumped from her chair.

"Quick, let's tidy up and do the dishes," she said.

Thomas and Margot stacked the plates and gathered the knives and spoons. Mother ran to the kitchen to get the dishwater ready.

"What's going on?" Father asked.

"There's people coming," said Thomas.

Father absently closed the Bible. "People? What people?"

But Margot and Thomas were already in the hallway. Father stood up and went after them into the kitchen.

"Quick, quick, quick," Mother called. "I still have to get changed!"

Suds splashed around merrily.

"What people?" asked Father.

"Aunt Pie," said Thomas.

"Perhaps you could push the table over to one side and arrange the chairs in a circle," said Mother.

"Just for Pie?" Father asked anxiously.

"Of course not," said Mother. "There are a lot more people coming."

"But who?" said Father. His voice was getting louder. "It isn't anybody's birthday, is it?"

"Friends of mine," said Mother. "Quick, quick, quick, perhaps you would like to get changed too?"

"Why haven't I heard about this before?" Father exclaimed. "Why doesn't anybody tell me anything?"

"Sorry, Papa," said Margot. "Forgot." She was drying the carving knife.

Father watched as she put the dried knife in the drawer.

"Yes, sorry," said Mother. "It completely slipped my mind."

"Sorry, Papa," said Thomas. "I meant to tell you, but then I suddenly had to go to the bathroom and then . . ."

"How many chairs should I put out?" Father asked.

"A dozen or so, I think," said Mother.

"TWELVE?" Father looked at her, aghast. "Where did you suddenly get TWELVE friends from?"

"Margot and Thomas and you and I will want a seat too," said Mother.

"EIGHT? EIGHT FRIENDS?"

But Mother did not respond anymore. She handed the dishwashing brush to Margot. "Can you finish up?" she asked. "I really have to go and get changed."

She pushed past Father into the hallway and ran up the stairs. "The table over to the side and the chairs in a circle," she called once more.

"Eight friends," Father muttered.

"Mama is just guessing, you know," said Margot. "There could be more. Some of my friends are coming too."

"WHAT?" Father shouted.

With a lot of clattering, Margot stacked the plates in the cupboard. Thomas played a serenade on the saucepans. From the bedroom, Mother gave a performance of "Ev'ry Bud Is Springing Open, Ev'ry Blossom's Peeping Out."

"And what about ME?" Father called up the stairs. "Where am I supposed to go tonight?"

No one answered. Dejectedly, he went into the room and started tugging at the table. He dragged it into the back room and then arranged the chairs in birthday formation. "But it is nobody's birthday as far as I know," he complained.

"Who is making the coffee?" Mother called from upstairs.

"I will, Mama," Margot shouted back.

Then the doorbell rang. Thomas pulled the rope at the top of the stairs and the front door clicked open. It was Aunt Pie. "Halloo-oo!" she sang out. "We're here!" Two more ladies climbed up the stairs behind her.

"Leave the door open, Aunt Pie," called Margot. "There's more people coming."

The door stayed wide open.

"There you are, my boy," she puffed when she got to the top. She carried a white box into the kitchen. Then she got hold of Thomas and hugged him. "This is Aunt Magda." She indicated a huge flowery dress behind her.

"Oh," said Thomas.

"And that is Aunt Bea."

Aunt Magda and Aunt Bea shook his hand. They were brand-new aunts Thomas had never seen before. Aunt Bea had a gold tooth that glittered cheerfully when she laughed. And she laughed a lot.

They went into the room.

"There you are, man of God," Aunt Pie called to Father.

She went and kissed him. There were red spots on his cheeks from her lipstick. "You've met Magda and Bea, I think?"

"I haven't had the honor," said Father. Under the huge flowery dress, all sorts of things wobbled about while they shook hands. It did not escape Father's notice.

"Yes, you have," said Aunt Pie. "They come to all my birthdays. And what do you think of my slacks?"

She was wearing a pair of pale-blue slacks with a zipper on the side.

Father didn't think anything of it.

"Pie can carry it off," said Aunt Magda. "My bottom's too big for it."

Father didn't want to look at any bottoms, so he looked at the ceiling. It really needed painting. The ceiling, that is.

There was more noise on the stairs. *Thump-creak-thump-creak.* It was music to Thomas's ears. He ran into the hallway. It could possibly be someone with one old shoe and one new one. But more likely, it was someone with a leather leg. He pressed his back into the toilet door.

It was Eliza. She didn't notice him in the dark hallway. She went through into the room. "Hi, Eliza," he heard Margot call out. There was some bustling noise.

"Where is Thomas?" asked Eliza. "I want to sit next to him. Thomas is my friend."

All over Holland and the rest of the world, far into the

deepest tropical regions, every bud was springing open, every blossom peeping out.

"Oh, Jesus," whispered Thomas. "I am so happy." But now he really didn't dare go inside.

Thump-creak-thump-creak. "Oh, is that where you are, Thomas!" said Eliza. "Are you hiding from me?"

"Of course not," said Thomas.

"Come here," she said. She held out her hand. It was her good hand, with five whole fingers. Hand in hand, they walked into the room.

Fortunately, Father did not see them, because he was hidden behind Aunt Magda's big bottom.

"Let's see now," said Eliza. "We'd better sit somewhere where everybody doesn't fall over my leg." She looked around the circle. "There, by the window," she said.

They sat down. Her leather leg stuck out, but that did not matter, because she was out of everybody's way.

"Well," she said. "How do I look?"

"Lovely," said Thomas, because she was wearing a sky-blue dress with a white collar. "By the way, does your father play violin?" he asked.

Eliza looked surprised. "Yes," she said. "How did you know?"

Thomas shrugged. "I just know. And your mother sings really beautifully."

Now Eliza was really perplexed. She let go of his hand and put her arm around his shoulders. "You're a very special boy, did you know that?" she asked.

"I do, sort of," said Thomas shyly.

"Now I suddenly knew what Eliza knew," Thomas wrote in *The Book of Everything*. "She knew it, and so did I: what there is about me."

Margot and Aunt Pie were bringing around coffee. And cakes from Aunt Pie's white box. There was more noise on the stairs. "Go and see who it is," said Eliza. "I'll keep your chair for you."

Thomas went into the hallway. Mrs. van Amersfoort was there already with her portable gramophone. Behind her, four elderly ladies were coming up the stairs. The first of them was carrying a flat case that held the records.

"This is Thomas," said Mrs. van Amersfoort when they were all in the hallway. "He is not afraid of witches."

"Just as well," giggled the lady with the records.

"At least I won't have to be careful then," said the old lady with the bunch of flowers.

"At last, a real man," sighed the old lady who held a bottle of red cordial in each hand.

"I prefer them a little bit scared," said the last of them. "Keeps them in their place." She laughed loudly. That was a scary sight, because you could see her upper teeth even when she had her mouth shut. And you could see them even worse when she snapped her mouth open.

"That shouldn't be a problem for you," said Mrs. van Amersfoort tartly. "Will you take the gramophone inside, Thomas?"

They walked into the room in single file. There was a chattering and a cackling like nothing on earth. Aunt Bea and Aunt Magda and Aunt Pie and Mrs. van Amersfoort and Margot and Eliza and the four old ladies all talked at once and nobody could understand a word. But everybody was having a great time.

"Oh!" Mrs. van Amersfoort cried suddenly. "We nearly forgot about you!"

Father stood pressed against the sideboard, because there was almost no room behind Aunt Magda's bottom. Mrs. van Amersfoort tried to shake his hand around Aunt Magda.

"Can you reach?" Aunt Magda asked. She bent forward, sticking out her bottom.

Now Mrs. van Amersfoort could get hold of his hand over Aunt Magda's shoulder. "It's hot in here, isn't it?" she said. She let go of Father's hand and called, "Can we have a window open?"

"Good idea," Eliza called back. She jumped up smartly on her leather leg and pushed the window up. A fresh breeze blew into the house.

And then Mother appeared in the doorway. Because the window and the front door were both wide open, her dress flapped like a flag. "Hello, everybody," she said. Everyone looked at her and the chattering died down. Her dress was pale yellow, almost white, and narrow at the top, with a wide skirt. She had carefully put on lipstick. Her hair hung down loose over her shoulders.

Thomas had never seen her so beautiful. He looked at Father, to see if he'd noticed. Father did notice. His face became as red as the flowers on Aunt Magda's dress.

"Has everyone got coffee?" asked Mother.

Then the chattering broke out again. Thomas could not imagine there ever being silence again in the reading-aloud club.

10

They had all finished their cakes. Coffee cups and lemonade glasses were empty. Aunt Bea treated Father to a cigar and lit one herself. And then the great moment arrived.

The program began.

Item one: Thomas Klopper recites a poem by Annie M. G. Schmidt.

Thomas stood up. He started with Master Sweet who washed his feet in the aquarium. He knew the whole poem by heart.

When he had finished, there was loud applause.

The old lady with the teeth asked, "What do you want to be when you grow up, Thomas?"

And Thomas said, "Happy. I want to be happy."

Everyone thought that was a good idea.

But then, suddenly, Father said, "Give a proper answer, Thomas. What do you want to be when you grow up?"

"I wanted to be happy, and nothing else," Thomas wrote in *The Book of Everything*. "I searched my brain for a proper answer, but I didn't find anything."

"Only good-for-nothings and weaklings are happy," said Father. "Life is a struggle."

All the aunts and all Mrs. van Amersfoort's friends stared at him as if he had farted. And Mother nervously twisted a strand of her hair.

Thomas sat down and looked at his shoes. Eliza put her good hand over his.

"Have you faced many struggles in your life?" the lady with the teeth asked Father. "Were you in the Resistance? Are you a brave man? Do you protect your wife and children against the evil world? Do you stand up for the weak? Are animals in good hands with you?"

Bewildered, Father stared at her teeth. "Well . . ." he began.

"Item two on the program," called Mrs. van Amersfoort. "Music from the portable gramophone."

She turned the handle. "One of Eliza's records," she announced.

Music rushed into the room such as Thomas had never heard. A whole lot of instruments were hooting all at once and there was a banging of drums. At first he couldn't make heads or tails of it. But then a bright trumpet gained the upper hand over the others. The trumpet sang and giggled like a skipping angel. It was hard to keep your legs still, because they wanted to skip along.

"Louis Armstrong," Aunt Bea called out, flashing her gold tooth.

"Oo-ooh!" shouted Aunt Magda. She raised her hands in

the air and shook her upper body. The flowers on her dress bobbed like small boats on choppy water.

Mrs. van Amersfoort got up and handed Thomas the cover of the record. It showed a black man with a shiny trumpet at his mouth.

"That is a black man," said Thomas, amazed. Because he thought that black people lived on the small coins the children took to school every week for the Missions. And not on trumpets. "I have never seen a black person for real," he said.

"There are so many things in the world we have not seen," said Eliza. "For instance, I have never seen a Rolls-Royce for real."

"Isn't it fantastic music!" Aunt Pie shouted. There was some whipped cream on her upper lip. "It gives me the shivers."

"Where? Where?" called the old ladies.

"All over," laughed Aunt Pie. She ran her hands over her blouse and her slacks.

When the music stopped, Father got up. "I've still got a lot of work to do," he said. He squeezed between a couple of chairs to the door. Thomas hoped he would go to the side room without saying anything. But when he got to the door he turned. "And anyway, I have no desire to listen to heathenish black music," he said. "And to poems that sound like empty vessels."

"Tiddlyum, tiddlyum, tiddlyum-tum-tum," sang Margot.

Father looked at her.

Margot stopped singing. She looked back. She did not look angry, she did not look friendly, she just looked. There was nothing to be read in her eyes.

Then Thomas saw that her eyes started to shine like mirrors. Father looked into those mirrors and saw himself. Nobody saw what he saw, because he was the only one who could look straight into her eyes. He had to face it all alone.

"Margot was no longer afraid," Thomas wrote in *The Book of Everything*. "And I saw her become a witch before my very eyes."

The aunts and the old ladies started talking away happily as if it were a perfectly normal thing to happen. Nobody took any more notice of Father.

"Item three on the program!" called Mrs. van Amersfoort. "Thomas recites another poem by Annie M. G. Schmidt."

And Father just stood there. He stared helplessly into Margot's eyes. Thomas saw that he loved her. And him. And Mother. He saw that Father wanted to stay in the room, but wanted to get away at the same time.

Father was afraid of laughter and joy. He was particularly afraid of ridicule. He was afraid that someone would say that humans are descended from apes. Or that the earth is much older than four thousand years. Or that someone would ask where Noah got his polar bears from. Or that someone would swear. Father was terrified.

Mother looked back at him. *Come on, love,* she gestured. *Come and join us.*

He could not. He did not dare belong with people. He turned and locked himself in the side room.

Thomas saw things other people could not see. He did not know why this was, but it had always been like that. He saw Father clean through the wall. Behind his desk. Alone. Thomas had an awful feeling in his stomach. At first he thought he had swallowed a rhinoceros, but a moment later he understood that he was feeling sorry for his father.

He recited his poem and received his applause, but his mind was not there.

At eight o'clock he had to go to bed, because the following day was a school day. Downstairs, music and laughter went on for a long time. He tried to think about Eliza, and not about Father in the side room. That was difficult.

"I was hoping he was sitting in front of the window so he could think," he wrote in *The Book of Everything*. "And not on his knees with his eyes closed." But he knew better.

It had been a wonderful evening all the same. The door had been open and anyone could come in. They had listened to exciting music and amusing poems.

"Come on, love. Come and join us," Thomas whispered.

"What did you say?" asked a familiar voice.

Thomas couldn't keep his eyes open, he was so sleepy.

"I said, 'Come on, love, come and join us,'" he murmured.

"Okay," said Jesus. The Lord sat down on the edge of Thomas's bed.

"It was a great evening," said Thomas.

"I'm glad to hear it," said Jesus.

Then they were silent for a while. Downstairs, Louis Armstrong played his trumpet.

"Jesus?" asked Thomas.

"Yes, Thomas?"

"Can you help Papa?"

"I am afraid not."

It was a pity, but Thomas understood that some people are hard to redeem.

You couldn't ask the Lord Jesus for the impossible.

"Do you think Eliza will wait for me?"

"I would think so," said Jesus.

"Is it scary when she takes her leather leg off?"

"Of course not," said Jesus. "You've faced worse things."

That was true. In his young life, he had already seen quite a few scary things. A Bottombiter, Granddad's artificial teeth, a wooden spoon, a swollen nose, a carving knife, and a woman with outboard teeth. And even so he was going to be happy later.

"Because I am going to marry her, you see," said Thomas.

The Lord Jesus put a hand on his head and said, "You have my blessing."

Then Thomas fell asleep and Jesus ascended into Heaven.

The angels were waiting for Him anxiously, heaving deep sighs.

"How are things with Thomas?" one of them asked.

"Yes, how is he?" at least a hundred others asked in unison. They were all hopelessly in love with him, you know.

"He will be all right," said Jesus.

"Are You going to call him to You soon?" asked a pitch-black angel. "I would so much like to play trumpet for him."

"No," said the Lord Jesus. He smiled. "Anyway, none of you would have the slightest chance with Thomas."

"Why not?" the angels asked, appalled.

"None of you has a leather leg that creaks when you walk," He said.

That was too much for them. Every single one of them was extraordinarily beautiful, but none had a leather leg. You can't have everything.

This translation was edited by Cheryl Klein
and art directed by Elizabeth Parisi.
The text was set in Centaur MT, Voluta Script, and Franklin Gothic.
This book was printed and bound by Berryville Graphics in Virginia.
The manufacturing was supervised by Jaime Capifali.